Missing

MABEL

Missing
MABEL

A Curl Up and Dye Mystery

Nancy Mehl

BARBOUR
PUBLISHING

For more information about Nancy Mehl, please access the author's Web site at the following Internet address: www.nancymehl.com

Cover design: Faceout Studio, www.faceoutstudio.com

Published by Barbour Publishing, Inc., P.O. Box 719, Uhrichsville, OH 44683, www.barbourbooks.com

Our mission is to publish and distribute inspirational products offering exceptional value and biblical encouragement to the masses.

 Member of the
Evangelical Christian
Publishers Association

Printed in the United States of America.

DEDICATION

To my beautiful, talented granddaughter, Karissa. May God give you the desires of your heart. And may all your desires originate from *His* heart.

ACKNOWLEDGMENTS

My profound thanks go out to the following people: To Sandi Megli who answered all my "funeral home" questions without making me feel stupid. To my dear friend John Frye for sharing his love of with me. To Chris Guerrero for answering my "hair" questions. To Mike and Glenda Hemphill for their approval of some of my "deadly details." To my nephew, Gary Decker, for answering my stockbroker questions. To my fabulous editor, Ellen Tarver, who made this book much better. To Faye Spieker and Kim Woodhouse, my dear readers. To Frances for the dynamite. To my editor and friend, Susan Downs. To my wonderful agent, Janet Benrey. To Norman and Danny for their love and support. And most of all, to my Father who loves me every second of every day. It's all for You.

CHAPTER ONE

I ran my comb once more through Cecilia Westerbrook's bangs, fluffed them, and then sprayed them lightly with hair spray. Her soft, silver hair framed her face like a halo. "You look beautiful," I whispered. I stood back and took in the entire effect. Being a hairdresser has its rewards. It makes me feel great when my customers look their best.

"Is she about ready?"

Not realizing that someone had come into the room, I jumped involuntarily. My friend Paula stepped up next to me. "Her daughter will be here soon."

"I think we're ready to go. How does she look?"

Paula smiled. "You've done a wonderful job."

I patted Cecilia's shoulder. "It was an honor."

At this point in our conversation, it would have been polite for Cecilia to respond with some kind of compliment. But that wasn't going to happen. Her silence didn't bother me though. You see, Cecilia Westerbrook had been dead since Monday.

Paula stepped behind me and started to push the gurney out of the room.

"Wait a minute." As I handed her the photograph I'd used as a guide, I glanced at it one last time. Cecilia's kind face smiled up at me. This was a woman who had spent her life loving others. I prayed that I'd done her justice. As I looked at her picture, I felt that the twinkle in her eyes was just for me—a thank-you for my work on her behalf.

As the door swung shut behind Paula, I began packing up the kit I carry to my assignments. It includes all the essentials: curling iron, combs, picks, brushes, gel, hair spray, and special coloring sticks to cover dark roots or unwanted gray. I'd just closed the clasp on my large attaché when my cell phone rang. I put the kit down and grabbed my purse. Finding my phone before it quits ringing is one of the biggest challenges in my life. My purse has an inside pocket that's perfect for my phone, but I can't seem to remember to put it there. My absentmindedness left me digging through all the junk I'd thrown in my bag, hoping I could locate the phone before the caller was shuttled to voice mail. I'd chosen Chopin's funeral march as my ringtone. Although I take my job very seriously, this is my one humorous concession toward a job some people consider rather macabre. I don't see it that way at all. To me, what I do is a ministry.

Success! My fingers closed around the phone. I pulled it out and flipped it open. "Hello?" I said rather breathlessly. You'd have thought I just ran a mile.

"Hilde?" the voice on the other side crackled. "Mabel Winnemaker came back late yesterday. She's ready to style. Can you come by now, or are you busy?"

Gwen Cox from Druther's Funeral Home. She's a sweet woman who manages to balance out the mortuary director's rather nasty disposition. Ronald Druther is a third-generation mortician who probably would have been happier in another line of work. I'm not certain just what he really aspires to, but if our state prison in Lansing is ever in need of a new warden, I have the perfect guy for them.

I told Gwen I was on my way and hung up. Then I tossed the phone into my purse, realizing as soon as it left my fingers that I'd forgotten once again to put it in its special pocket.

Mabel Winnemaker. I'd stopped by Druther's early Monday morning to work on someone else and had accidentally run into Mabel when I turned right instead of left and wandered into the wrong room. A quick look told me that the woman lying on the table wasn't ready to get her hair done. I checked her identification tag and found her name, confirming that she was not the person I was looking for. I discovered my client in the room next door and was combing her out when Gwen came in. I probably should have mentioned my mistake, but since Druther's is a fairly new account for me, I didn't want to sound like someone who couldn't follow simple instructions.

That's when Gwen mentioned that Mabel wouldn't need my services until after she came back from the coroner's office.

Something about Mabel's grandson requesting an autopsy. Druther's had been forced to delay the embalming, and Mabel and I had to put off our official introduction for a couple of days. That was okay with me. It wasn't like she was late for our appointment because she'd found something better to do.

I hoped there wasn't anything suspicious about her death. I have a hard time working with clients who meet their demise through unnatural causes. It's emotionally draining and requires a lot of prayer. Because of the unusual circumstances, I'd only gotten a peek at Mabel before she was taken away. I saw nothing that concerned me. She was quite elderly and had probably died from a condition brought on by old age. From that one quick glance at her hair, I could see that she definitely needed a touch-up around the roots. However, I didn't look at her face. Usually I only see clients after they have been prepared by the mortuary staff. It's easier that way. I'd kept my eyes trained on the only part that required my services.

I glanced at my watch. I was supposed to meet my mother at one o'clock. Just enough time to do Mabel's hair and get to the restaurant. Lunch with Mother. Not something I looked forward to. My mother still couldn't understand why I'd left college to go to beauty school and ended up working on "dead people's hair, for crying out loud." Mom is a successful neurosurgeon who is absolutely horrified by my career choice. I'd tried once to explain to her how it happened, but her dazed look told me that she was either taking a quick, open-eyed nap, or she was thinking about the next skull she planned to crack open. At least we were both concentrating on the same end of the body.

No matter how I tried to express myself when it came to my present job, she couldn't understand it. To be honest, I wasn't exactly certain myself how it happened. Fresh out of beauty school and accepted into one of the top salons in Wichita, I was in a position to make good money while doing something I thought I would really enjoy. I knew my mother had pulled some strings to get me hired by Monsieur Maximilian, who owned Maximilian's Salon de L'Élégance. Although it's the premier salon in the city, I was *L'Miserable*. Most of my clients were rich, older women who wanted to look like Julia Roberts. When they stared into a mirror and saw crow's feet, double chins, and loose skin, somehow it was always my fault. My hairstyles were supposed to perform miracles, it seemed. Unfortunately, God didn't see fit to fill my combs and brushes with miracle-working power.

My life changed one afternoon about a year ago when Monsieur Max grabbed the back of my coat and screeched, "Ah, *ma petite chérie*, you must grab your combs and go right now!"

Assuming I was fired, I felt an overwhelming sense of relief. However, that was followed by a rush of terror when I understood that I was being sent to a local funeral home to fix the hair of a recently departed patron. The family insisted that their dear mother's hair be styled by the same salon that had been taking care of her for years. Surprisingly, no one else wanted to go. Feeling that my career, such as it was, was hanging by a thread, I drove to The Sweet Slumberland Funeral Home, shaking like a leaf. I was scared stiff (no pun intended) as I was led down the hall to my client. But once we were alone, something happened to me. I felt a real peace in that room, and before long, Gertrude's hair was beautifully coiffed.

A couple of days later, I slipped quietly into the back of the church where her funeral was being held. Because she and her family were well known in the community, the church was packed and no one noticed me. After the service, I followed the procession of mourners who filed past her open casket. Two women in front of me stopped to stare at their late friend.

"Oh my goodness," one whispered to the other. "She looks lovely. She always had the most beautiful hair."

"Yes she did," the other acknowledged. "Her daughter was worried that her mother wouldn't look right. Gertie was very fastidious, you know. But I understand Carol was so comforted when she saw her mother at the funeral home, she broke down and cried with relief. I'm glad she'll be able to remember Gertrude this way."

Anyone seeing me would have thought Gertrude Maitland and I were close friends. Maybe the tears I wept weren't from a relationship with the elderly woman while she was alive, but we still had a bond. She had needed me to help her say good-bye. As I stood over her casket, I realized that

I'd found something I wanted to do. I could use my skills with clients who wouldn't be voicing silly complaints, while I brought comfort to grieving families. I'd accidentally found my calling. I hurried back to the salon and quit my job that very afternoon. After listening to a stream of French phrases I'm pretty sure were dancing on the edge of profanity, I said good-bye to Monsieur Max, who was actually raised in Boise, Idaho, and set off on my new venture. Within two weeks I had work. After a couple of jobs, the word spread quickly throughout the mortuary community. Even homes with their own cosmetologists called me. Applying makeup to the faces of the deceased was one thing. Fixing their hair is quite another. It took a level of skill most mortuary employees don't have. One thing that helps me tremendously is that I always ask for a picture of my client so I can style their hair the same way they wore it when they were alive. I still remembered my great-aunt Edna's service. Her long hair, which was always worn in a bun, had been cut and tightly curled. She didn't look at all like herself. My grandmother was devastated.

"I don't know who that is," she'd declared at the viewing, "but that is certainly not my sister!"

I was determined that would never happen at one of my funerals.

I made it to Druther's in plenty of time, even though an overnight storm had dumped about three inches of snow on Wichita streets. A small snowplow was clearing the parking lot when I pulled in. Many businesses hired private firms to keep their lots clean. Funeral homes deal with a lot of elderly people. Making it safe for them is of utmost importance. I was pretty happy to find a space fairly close to the door that had already been plowed, although I left the closest spaces for clients. I certainly felt much more fortunate than the driver of a black van in the alley on the west side of the building. The plow had formed a wall of snow in front of him. Either he'd have to push through or wait for the plow to clear it away.

Walking in through the front door of a funeral home is always the same. Lots of wood, plush carpeting, and the feeling that you should whisper. Just once, I want to walk into a mortuary decorated with clowns and rainbows. Okay, maybe not clowns. Frankly they frighten me. Always have. I'm convinced that sometime during my childhood I'd been frightened by some kind of renegade killer clown. Not that there are many renegade killer clowns. Well, there was John Gacy, but I'd never lived anywhere near him.

I also hate orange. With a passion. Maybe I'd once been chased by an orange renegade killer clown. Who knows? Years ago, I'd asked my mother why I'm afraid of clowns and the color orange, but she'd just looked at me like I was in desperate need of immediate therapy and changed the subject. That happens a lot with my mother. We have very little in common. Mom is tall, sleek, and blond. She reeks classy. Unfortunately, I seem to reek something entirely different. My natural hair color is somewhere between the color in the washing machine after you throw your muddy jeans in the water and the edges of a plant that is slowly but surely giving up the ghost. I've had lots of experience with both of those scenarios, by the way.

About six months ago, I'd had enough. I cut off my unruly hair, settling for a short, straight style that takes about thirty seconds to comb. I also traded my weird brownish color for something entirely different. I dyed my hair black except for my bangs and one streak on the side, both of which are now a lovely shade of magenta. I love it. Of course every now and then, a glance at my reflection makes me wonder what in the world I've done, but since Mom hates it so much, I'm in for the long haul. I try to stay as far away from mirrors as possible anyway. In my opinion, my eyes are too far apart, my forehead is too high, and my mouth is too big. All in all, everything about me is just *too* something. Being over the top seems to be my *spécial* gift, as Max from Boise used to say. A little mascara in the morning, a brush through my hair a couple times a day, and I'm good to go.

"Hilde, there you are."

I have a propensity for daydreaming. Gwen's greeting snapped me back to reality.

"Hello, Gwen," I said, keeping my tone as funereal as possible. No rainbows or killer clowns today. "I have about an hour for Mrs. Winnemaker. Will that be enough?"

"Should be plenty of time. I've got to grab the file, and then I'll introduce you." She turned and hurried into her office.

Before I had a chance to follow, someone else poked his head out of one of the rooms.

"Hey there, Hilde!"

Eddie Hanson, one of Druther's salesmen, had a big, squirrelly grin plastered on his sallow face. He has a way of staring at me that gives me the creeps. I try to remember the scripture admonishing us to love everyone, but it's difficult in Eddie's case. I'm not proud of my lack of charity toward him.

"Hi, Eddie. Sorry I can't talk now. I'm running a little late today."

"That's okay. Why don't you stop by on your way out?"

"We'll see. Can't promise anything. See you later." I tried to duck into Gwen's office, cutting off further conversation. To my surprise, the door was locked. I could almost feel Eddie's beady little eyes locked on me. I knocked sharply on the door.

After a few seconds, it opened. "Sorry. It must have accidentally latched behind me," Gwen said, her face flushed. "I'm still looking for the file. I can't imagine what I did with it."

I smiled at her. "Relax. You're too organized to have actually lost it. I'll bet it's here somewhere." The chill in the room drew my attention to her back door, which stood slightly ajar. I pointed it out.

"Thanks, Hilde. Guess I forgot to close it after I dumped the trash." She locked the door with a sigh. "It's been a busy day, and it isn't even noon yet."

Gwen's office reflects her personality. Soft pastel colors,

delicate flowers on the wallpaper, and a small, indoor water fountain create a feeling of peace and tranquility. No wonder clients feel comfortable with her. Even though her primary job is that of office manager, Mr. Druther also uses her to meet with grieving families, tacking on the title of "funeral consultant" to her name. Smart move. Gwen has a way of getting people to relax and share their concerns. Ron Druther, on the other hand, is all business, always seems stressed, and has a smile that reminds me of a baby with gas.

"Oh, by the way," Gwen said, rifling through a file drawer, "we'll need you again on Friday. We have a viewing set up for the weekend."

I set my bag on one of the chairs facing her desk and pulled out my schedule book. I opened to Friday. "I can be here by ten thirty. Will that work for you?"

"That will be fine, Hilde," she said with a smile.

I picked up a pen lying on the edge of her desk and wrote the appointment in my notebook. I'm not saying I'm scatter-brained, but I learned long ago that if I wait too long to put dates on my schedule, I tend to forget them. A couple of unfortunate incidents early in my career taught me a lesson I had no intention of repeating.

"Eureka!" Gwen squealed, waving a file in the air. "Here it is. Guess I accidentally picked it up when I was putting another file away."

I barely had time to grab my satchel before she swept through the door and down the hall with Mabel's information in her hand. I trotted quickly behind her in an attempt to catch up as she headed toward a set of double wooden doors that were usually kept locked. Plush carpeting, classy wallpaper with proper muted tones, and low-volume new age music gave way to cheap, low-fiber covered floors and drab, whitewashed walls. This was the section of the mortuary reserved for those who didn't care anymore about decor or melodious accompaniment.

Gwen pointed to the door at the end of the hall where my client waited. I paid special attention. I had no intention of getting the wrong room this time. "She's in there. Here's the picture from the family." She put the file on top of a nearby table and opened it. I watched as she shuffled the papers out of the way and found a photo in the back of the folder. She pulled it out and handed it to me. "There isn't going to be a viewing. Mabel's grandson won't be here in time for the service. He lives overseas." She shook her head. "The casket will be closed during the funeral. I guess it was Mabel's wish. But she still needs to look as nice as possible. You know the routine."

I did. It's always better to prepare the body for viewing in case someone in the family changes their mind. A lot of people convince themselves that they don't want to see their loved one dead, lying in a casket, preferring to remember them as they appeared when they were alive. But when it actually comes time to say good-bye, the reality causes them to desire one more look. Mabel would be as beautiful as we could make her in case that happened.

I glanced down at the picture and saw a woman whose face was almost completely hidden by one of the ugliest dogs I'd ever seen. "What is this?"

"I believe it's a pug," Gwen said.

"I'm not asking about the dog. Is this the best picture you could get?"

"Unfortunately, yes. Mrs. Winnemaker was being cared for by a nephew who couldn't find any other picture except this one. She'd only been with him and his wife for a couple of years."

"In two whole years, no one took a better picture of her? Yikes."

"Well, at least you can see how she wore her hair. That's the most important thing, isn't it?"

Gwen's smile and cheery tone made me feel better. "Yes, I guess so. Doing her makeup must have been tough, though."

"Not really. Mrs. Winnemaker didn't wear any cosmetics. We just did the basics." Gwen patted my shoulder. "No special problems with this one. Mabel died peacefully in her sleep of old age." She smiled. "I'll leave you to it. I know you'll do your usual, inspired job."

I nodded, hoping she was right. Gwen turned and made her way back to the land of the living while I headed down the hall to reacquaint myself with the dead. Although Mabel and I had met briefly a couple of days earlier, now we would be spending some quality time together.

I leaned against the swinging metal doors and entered a large room with cement floors. Equipment used for embalming, along with closets and shelves full of supplies, waited in darkened corners. But a bright light illuminated the spot where Mabel waited silently for me. She had already been dressed. Styling her hair was the last step in the process before she was settled into her coffin and prepared for viewing. I liked being the last link in the chain. It gave me a chance to make certain everything was in place. More than once, I'd called mortuary staff in to correct something that didn't look right: smeared makeup, twisted ties, missing body parts. The last situation had only occurred once. The family had sent over their father's prosthetic arm, but it hadn't been attached. Major faux pas. Most mortuary staff really appreciate it when I catch mistakes. Sloppy funeral homes don't last long in a surprisingly competitive business.

Mabel's silver locks were clean and spread out behind her. A client's hair is always washed by the funeral home before it's styled. Washing the body and the hair helps to make certain that any lingering germs and bacteria are removed. In some cases it's also necessary to remove blood, but thankfully Mabel hadn't died violently. Gwen had confirmed that she'd simply passed away in her sleep. A good way to go when you're eighty-seven.

I was still a little puzzled as to why someone had asked for an autopsy, but since it had nothing to do with me, I pushed the thought out of my mind. I needed to concentrate on the part of Mabel's care that *was* my business.

I grabbed a pair of surgical gloves from my kit and pulled them on. Then I prayed. I always pray before starting my work. I ask for God's help to honor the person entrusted to my care. I also pray for the family. It helps me feel like I'm a part of their healing process instead of a stranger who is intruding in their time of grief.

As soon as I began to comb her hair, I knew something was terribly wrong. I remembered Mabel's hair. It was fine and soft and had needed a little color around the roots. That was something I did a lot in this job. A prolonged illness usually keeps people from running down to their favorite beauty salon for a touch-up. Though this hair looked almost the same, but it was much coarser and the ends were split. Also, the color was naturally white—all the way down to the roots.

Even though I couldn't tell by looking at her face, I knew beyond a shadow of a doubt that the woman lying on the table in front of me was not Mabel Winnemaker.

CHAPTER TWO

Miss Higgins, Druther's Funeral Home is not in the practice of mixing up bodies. I assure you that we take special care to correctly identify our clients. I've checked our files and two different sets of tags. I can say without any reservations that the woman you are referring to is indeed Mrs. Mabel Winnemaker."

Ronald Druther has one of those veins in his temple that sticks out when he's upset. At the moment, it looked like it was in danger of exploding. My plan wasn't to give him a stroke. I simply wanted to warn him about a serious mix-up.

"I accidentally walked into the wrong room the other day when I was here, Mr. Druther," I said as soothingly as possible, keeping my eye on his throbbing temple. "Unless the identification was wrong, I definitely saw Mabel Winnemaker. Could her paperwork have been wrongly placed with another body? Is that possible?"

"Absolutely not. Mrs. Winnemaker is the only elderly, Caucasian female we've had since Monday. Our only other clients are Mr. Gonzalez and Mr. Nguyen. I trust you haven't confused them with Mrs. Winnemaker?"

"No, Mr. Druther. I can tell the difference between a man and a woman." Of course, with my limited experience in that department, anything is possible, but that wasn't something I was prepared to admit. One thing I *did* know was hair, and the woman lying in the back room was *not* the person I'd seen on Monday. "Can't you call her family and ask them to identify the remains? I'm sure they can tell you that this woman isn't Mabel Winnemaker."

"I have no intention of causing the family that kind of stress," he said, his voice sharp. He picked up Mabel's file, which was lying on his desk, and rifled through it. "They've requested a closed casket. That tells me they're not interested in seeing her. To ask them to view the body under these circumstances is out of the question."

He sighed heavily and ran his hand over the top of his head. I would have said that he ran his hand through his hair, but there isn't much up there. Ronald Druther is a short, foppish man with thick glasses, whose entire being seems to suggest resignation. Now he wanted me to resign myself to something I knew wasn't true. My stubborn personality made it a pretty sure bet that wasn't going to happen.

"Are you going to do the job we've hired you to do, Miss Higgins? Or do I need to ask someone else to complete your duties?"

I started to tell him that I had no intention of getting

involved in something that was probably going to end up being the biggest mess Druther's had ever stepped in, but at the last second I thought of Mabel—and whoever that was waiting for me in the back room. My well-worn conscience wouldn't allow me to abandon either one of them. "I'll finish the job, Mr. Druther. I just thought you'd like to know that you're making a huge mistake. What you do with that information is your business. I've told you the truth. It's out of my hands."

I left his office wondering if I could simply finish this assignment and walk away. Ronald Druther might not have to pay the price for his incompetence, but what about Mabel? What about the woman lying on that gurney? And what about their families?

I needed to talk to someone who could give me some good advice. I went back to the room where the fake Mabel waited and searched for my phone. I found it and punched in Paula's work number. It only took a few rings before she answered. I quickly explained my dilemma.

"Jumpin' Jehosaphat, Hilde. Are you sure it's not the same body?"

"Absolutely certain. And Mr. Druther won't listen to me. I don't know what to do."

The silence coming from the other end told me Paula was thinking hard. I could almost hear the gears turning in her head. I waited, hoping her experience in the business end of dying would guide my next move.

Finally she said, "I'm not certain what to tell you. It's not like this happens a lot." She paused for a few seconds more and then sighed. "Look, why don't you go ahead and finish your work? Your client's not going anywhere. Hopefully the family will change their minds and take a peek at her. Then everything will be cleared up, and you won't have to be in the middle. Call me later today. I'll do whatever I can to help."

"Okay, I will. Thanks for being there."

"Oh—I almost forgot," Paula said. "I have a new cell phone number. Do you have a way to write it down?"

I grabbed my purse. "Yes. Give me a second." I put the phone down on the counter and located a small notebook I always carry with me. Then I selected one of the miscellaneous pens that are always floating around in the bottom of my purse. The first one I grabbed came from one of the local grocery stores. I chose it over the pen I accidentally pilfered from my bank and a pen from an out-of-town hotel I've never stayed in. I have a propensity for acquiring other people's writing instruments. I don't mean to do it, and I valiantly try to return all of them to their rightful owners. But quite a few remain mysteries forever. Like the nice ballpoint from The Pigeon Roost Bar and Grill in Ash Flat, Arkansas. I've never set foot in Arkansas. Everyone has a talent, I guess. Mine is collecting pens that don't belong to me. It probably won't land me a spot on *America's Got Talent*. But I might have a chance with *America's Most Wanted*.

As I picked up my phone, I heard a noise. I jerked so hard

I almost dropped the phone on the floor. I looked around the darkened room. Although there were lots of places someone could hide, I didn't see anyone. I let out a nervous giggle. My imagination had shifted into overdrive, and I purposefully pushed away a growing feeling of paranoia.

"Okay, I'm ready," I said into the phone. I scribbled down the number and dumped the notepad and pen into my purse.

"Hilde," Paula said slowly, "are you absolutely sure about this? If you cause a big stink and you're wrong. . ."

"I'm not wrong, Paula. I don't know who this woman is, but she's not the same woman I saw two days ago. If I wasn't certain, I wouldn't say anything."

"Okay, I believe you. You have your camera, don't you?"

I'd started carrying a camera several months ago, after a mortuary staff member took it upon herself to redo one of my clients. The family wasn't happy with the outcome, and I had no way to prove that the result wasn't my work. Now I take pictures when I'm done so I have a little insurance against overly helpful, amateur hairdressers. Most people would have considered my collection of clients' photos a rather ghoulish display, but I only keep the pictures until the funeral is over. After that, I delete them.

I assured Paula that I would definitely take a few snapshots before I left, thanked her, and hung up. Then I got to work styling my mystery woman's hair. I used the picture with the dog as a guide, but it was difficult. Hair doesn't grow straight out of the head. We all have parts and waves that a good hair-stylist will attempt to work with. Trying to get hair to do something unnatural can produce less than satisfying results. The fake Mabel's hair didn't want to be shaped exactly like the picture. Eventually I got it as close as possible and put my combs, brushes, curling iron, and hair spray back in my attaché. I glanced down at my watch. Yikes! It was almost twenty till one. I was going to be late meeting my mother. That would certainly get things started off in the wrong direction. Mom hates it when anyone is late—especially me. She claims that stealing her time is just as bad as stealing her property.

As fast as I could, I took several pictures, particularly of the woman's face. Then I packed everything up and set it next to the door. Although I didn't want to take the time, nature loudly called my name. The culprit was my affinity for coffee. I ran down the hall to find the ladies' room occupied. I had to wait several minutes for my turn. Once inside, I took care of business as quickly as I could. Then I washed my hands and checked myself in the mirror. My hair needed brushing before I met my mother, but since my purse was still in the other room, I decided to take care of it once I got in the car.

I hurried back to get my things and say good-bye to the woman who lay waiting for someone to discover she was missing. To my surprise, I almost ran into Ron Druther and Gwen in the hallway.

Ron frowned when he saw me. "In these circumstances, I

feel it's necessary to check your work. I hope you understand."

I didn't, but I nodded anyway. "I don't mind at all, Mr. Druther. I want you to be happy."

We entered the room together. I watched while he inspected my efforts. "Everything looks fine," he said slowly. He sounded disappointed.

"Thank you." I picked up my bag. Actually, it bothered me that he'd felt the need to make certain I hadn't shaved the woman's head or dyed her hair pink. Up until this moment, I'd built up a reputation of trust with my clients. I recognized that this situation could ruin future jobs at Druther's. But I intended to do what was right—no matter the consequences.

As I turned to leave, I realized that I still had the photo Gwen had given me. I glanced at it one more time before handing it back to her. Although I couldn't see my client's facial features, her dog stared straight into my eyes. He might have been ugly, but the look on his face was one of pure joy. This was a happy dog. I wondered where he was now and if someone was taking good care of him. Thinking about that dumb dog brought tears to my eyes. It had been a stressful morning. Hopefully the rest of the day would be better.

I was almost out the front door when I heard someone yell my name. Ron marched down the hall toward me, his face the color of ripe beets. If it had been possible, smoke might have poured out of his ears.

"Miss Higgins," he hissed. "I think you need to come

with me." He grabbed me and began pulling me toward his office.

I wrestled my arm away from his viselike grip. "Excuse me, Mr. Druther," I said loudly. "I don't like being manhandled. If something's wrong, I would appreciate it if you would address me like an adult. What in heaven's name is the problem?"

By this time, several people had stepped out of their offices, and Gwen had rushed up behind the enraged funeral director. My old friend Eddie poked his head out of his office, too, but his expression was almost jubilant, as if my predicament was providing him some kind of twisted entertainment.

"I would appreciate it if you would step into my office where we can talk about this in private." Mr. Druther pushed each word out as if it were painful for him.

I turned on my heel and headed for his office, feeling embarrassed, humiliated, and a little angry. I glanced at Gwen. Her face was pale, and her large eyes were locked on mine. I looked at her questioningly, but she just stood there, staring at me like she'd never seen me before. Mr. Druther closed the door behind us.

"Sit down, Miss Higgins," he said sharply. "I'm afraid we have a situation."

"I know, Mr. Druther," I said, choosing to stand. "I already told you that. You've got the wrong body."

He slapped the top of his desk with force. "I'm not talking about your ridiculous allegations—something you obviously made up to cover your real agenda."

I had the strange feeling that I was speaking one language and he was conversing in another. A line from an old Paul Newman movie popped into my head: *"What we got here is a failure to communicate."* I finally sat down out of frustration. "I have no idea what you're talking about. You're going to have to spell it out for me, I'm afraid."

He shook his head, his jaw and the vein in his head working overtime in an attempt to deal with the stress of the situation. Not that I knew what the situation was. "Miss Higgins," he said, enunciating each word as if he were speaking to a rather slow child. "I would like to know what you did with Mrs. Winnemaker's diamond wedding ring. It is missing, and *you* are the last person to attend to her. I want that ring back now." He hit his desk again, causing me to jump. "And I mean *right now!*"

To say I was shocked is an understatement. To infer that I would ever steal anything from one of my clients is like accusing me of hiding Osama bin Laden. My relationship with the people I work with is a sacred trust to me. I would never betray it.

"I can assure you, Mr. Druther, I don't have anyone's diamond ring. I'm not a thief, and I am appalled that you would accuse me of something like that." I tried to keep my voice steady, but it shook with emotion.

"If you're innocent, then you won't mind if I check your carrying case?"

I picked up my attaché and set it on the desk in front of

him. "Have at it."

He rifled through it for several minutes, taking out my styling implements and then putting them back. He scowled with frustration after finding nothing incriminating.

"Now your purse, please?" I wondered just how far he planned to push this. I could guarantee him that the only cavities he would be searching were the ones inside my bags. Anything else was off-limits.

I grabbed my purse and proceeded to dump its contents on his desk. About the only thing he would see that could cast aspersions on my character were those stupid pens, but I seriously doubted he would be concerned about something from The Pigeon Roost Bar and Grill.

What he was interested in, however, was a rather large, sparkling diamond wedding band that bounced out of my purse, rolled across the desk, and came to rest right in front of him.

CHAPTER THREE

"Oh for heaven's sake, Hilde. I told you that silly job was going to be trouble. Why can't you listen to good advice when it's offered to you?"

As predicted, lunch had started off with a bang. Being thirty minutes late wasn't the main course in my mother's attempt to make me eat crow. The pièce de résistance was the recounting of my humiliation and expulsion from Druther's Funeral Home. Mr. Druther had banned me from ever darkening their doors again. He'd also threatened to inform the other mortuaries in town about my penchant for pilfering from the recently perished. He informed me that the only reason he wasn't going to call the police was because he didn't want Druther's to be known as a place where their clients weren't protected from "people like you." I wanted to ask him if he meant *hairdressers,* but I didn't think he would have appreciated my attempt at humor. I also wanted to ask him if his clients would like to know that even though their loved one's possessions would now be protected, their actual loved ones might not be.

"My *silly job* has nothing to do with this, Mother." I hated the whiny tone in my voice, but I *felt* whiny. "Doctors get accused of ripping people off, too. You just hide it by calling it *fees*."

"Hildegarde Bernadette Higgins," my mother sputtered. "I do not *rip people off*, as you so eloquently put it. I'm worth every penny I charge and more. I save people's lives."

Although I've never been certain what "hackles" were, my mother's use of my full name raised mine to attention. High on painkillers after my birth and recently inspired by the lives of two nuns she'd been reading about, Mother had given me a name I couldn't spell until the second grade. Her fascination with these dead saints eventually moved on, but my unfortunate moniker stayed behind.

In an attempt to calm my excited hackles, I forced myself to focus on the overpriced menu at Wichita's newest restaurant, The Nantucket Beach Club. This was haute cuisine at its goofiest. First of all, Nantucket may have beaches, but Wichita, Kansas, certainly does not. Trust me, Wichita has very little in common with New England. But whatever. It's the new hot spot in a city already overburdened with restaurants.

Before I had a chance to look over the entire menu, our waiter, who had introduced himself earlier as Clive, sashayed up to the table. I ordered the Free-Range Curried Chicken Salad. Mother ordered something in French. Since those same words had never dripped from Monsieur Max's lips, I didn't understand her, but the waiter nodded as if he'd spent his entire life in Paris. Dutifully impressed by my mother's charms, he promised to make certain the chef paid special attention to *our* order. Fat chance. Clive was only aware of one person at our table. I could suddenly grow lobster claws, turn green, and sprout asparagus out of my ears, and he wouldn't even notice. It's been that way all my life; I'm used to it. Clive hurried away to deliver Mom's order to the kitchen. I could only hope he wouldn't drop mine on the floor and forget to pick it up.

"Never mind, Mother," I said after our love-struck waiter beat his hasty retreat. "I probably shouldn't have dumped this on you, but I'm really upset. I think someone planted that ring so I would quit asking questions about Mabel Winnemaker."

"Hilde, could you have accidentally picked the ring up? Or could it have fallen into your purse by mistake?" My mother raised her perfectly formed nose a notch. "I mean, your handbag *is* a disaster."

"Even so, I think I'd notice a stray diamond ring." I had no intention of admitting it, but her comment caused a seed of doubt to sprout in my mind. Was it possible? Could I have transferred my pen-pinching skills to valuable jewelry? I turned the idea over in my head a couple of times before I dismissed it as impossible.

"Wait a minute," I said more to myself than to anyone else. I looked at my mother because she was the only other person at the table. "There wasn't any jewelry on the body. It hadn't been placed yet. There was no way for me to get my hands on it, even if I'd wanted to."

"You could have stolen it from a drawer or something," Mother offered helpfully.

"Well, thank you for that vote of confidence, but may I remind you that I'm not actually a thief?" Well, there was the pen thing, but that was out of my control. I decided not to count it. "The thing is, Druther's doesn't apply the jewelry until after the hair is done. And until it's needed, it's kept in a safe with tags tied to each piece. That way, nothing gets mixed up."

"Seems they should be just as careful with their bodies," my mother said dryly.

I sneaked a quick look at her. Was she serious? Did she believe me, or was she tempted by a good one-liner she couldn't resist? I wasn't certain.

"The ring wasn't even on the body," I repeated. "I should have realized it right away, but I was so upset I didn't think of it until now."

"Is that the way it's always done?" Mom asked as if she didn't really want to know.

"No. Different mortuaries have different procedures. Some of them want the styling done before the body is dressed. I don't like that. The hair can get messed up. But Druther's always asks me to do the hair after the dressing. Their last step is to apply the jewelry and anything else the family wants in the casket."

"Okay, okay. I don't need to know any more than that." She shivered. "It's gruesome, and it certainly isn't proper lunch conversation."

"Let me get this straight," I said sarcastically. "You pop people's heads open several times a week and fiddle around inside their brains, but what I do is too distasteful to discuss? That makes perfect sense."

"It's different," she sniffed. "My patients are all *alive*. It's not the same thing at all."

I reached for a roll. My stomach was beginning to rumble with hunger. I figured it wouldn't be much longer. Clive and his testosterone-loaded kitchen buddies had probably put everyone else's order on hold so that Mommy Dearest wouldn't have to wait too long for her Grilled Salmon Nicoise, or whatever she'd ordered. "Surely not all your patients have survived, Mother," I said, spitting out a few bread crumbs on the tablecloth.

My mother's face turned ashen, and she reached for her herbal tea. "It's impossible to save everyone, Hilde. You know that."

"Of course I do. I deal with the aftermath of your failures every day. What do you think? That your patients who die just go *poof* and disappear? People like me take care of them when you're finished." As soon as the last word left my mouth, I realized how cruel my comment was. My mother looked absolutely stricken.

"I. . .I don't believe any such thing, Hilde," she said

in a low voice, her eyes darting around the room, looking everywhere except at her heartless daughter.

What was wrong with me? I'd turned into the daughter from *The Bad Seed*—only not as cheery. "I'm sorry, Mother." I reached across the table and grabbed her wrist. "I truly am. I wasn't thinking. This has been a really rotten day."

She yanked her arm out of my grasp and smoothed her Oscar de la Renta tweed skirt. Then she straightened her charcoal gray cashmere sweater. "I'm sorry, Hilde, but I think you meant every word of it. For some reason, we seem to bring out the very worst in each other." She peered at me through narrowed eyes. Her colored contacts made her irises an unearthly blue. "I have no plan to apologize to you for working hard and being successful. My career supported us very well after your father took off with his tax attorney. I could have tried to find him—asked him for alimony or child support, but I didn't. I took care of us without his help, and if I take my career seriously now, it's because sometimes I feel it's all I have."

I felt about two inches high. I'd been asking God to heal the deep wounds between my mother and me, but His job was cut out for Him today. I seemed to be doing everything I could to make our division even more profound.

"You have me, Mother," I said quietly. "I'm just so freaked out about this situation, I've been taking it out on you. That's not fair." I took a deep breath. Might as well go all the way. I was hanging out there pretty far already. "I'm not completely clueless, you know. I'm fully aware that a lot of our problems in the past have been my fault. I'll try harder. I really will." I felt tears start to fill my eyes. I blinked them away but not fast enough.

"All right, Hilde. Maybe we both need to put out some effort." She sighed and crossed her arms. "I truly don't understand your decision to pursue this. . .this. . .thing you do. You were in college, and everything seemed to be going well. Then suddenly you quit."

"We've been over this many times. You know why. It just wasn't for me."

"I know, I know. Let's not rehash it." She cleared her throat and took another sip of tea. "I pushed you too hard. I'm aware of that." She set her cup down and gave me a strained smile. "You've come to me with this problem. Let's see if I can help. Is there anything else you can tell me?"

I'd just started to discuss my options when the food came. Clive *presented* my mother's food to her with a flourish. He plopped my salad in front of me without even glancing my way. I waited for him to leave then bowed my head and prayed silently over my food.

"Are you still doing that in public?" my mother whispered after looking around to see if any of her high-society friends had seen me.

I pretended not to hear her. This is one of our ongoing disputes. My mother feels that praying in front of other people is inappropriate. She likes to tell me that God doesn't appreciate public displays. I, on the other hand, like to respond by quoting the scripture in Luke about being ashamed of Christ in front of other people. We're probably both a little right and both a little wrong. It's an argument neither one of us will ever win.

My mother was still reeling from my decision to leave the church she'd brought me up in. I call it the "church of the frozen chosen." My new church home is more contemporary and expressive. Mother refers to it as "that happy clappy church." I don't really mind. We do clap, and I am really happy there.

Mother daintily picked at her food while I shoveled mine in with gusto. My table manners brought a sharp rebuke. "For goodness' sakes, Hilde. You eat everything like it's that . . . that. . ."

"It's called SPAM®, Mother," I said, loud enough for the people at the next table to hear. Their raised eyebrows indicated their shock that anyone in The Nantucket Beach Club would mention a canned-meat product in a place where the most down-to-earth menu selection is probably the one-hundred-dollar cheesesteak sandwich made with Kobe beef.

"I have never understood your enthusiasm for that. . . that. . ."

I opened my mouth to speak, but before I could say anything, my mother shushed me. "Don't say it," she hissed, almost spitting out her salmon.

My love for SPAM® products had certainly not come from

my mother. In fact, I was eighteen years old and out on my own before I ever tasted it. It quickly became my favorite food. My cupboards are always well stocked with different varieties and flavors. I've become so good at creating recipes with the great-tasting meat that I've entered the SPAM® recipe contest at the state fair the last two years. I won second place last September with my stuffed zucchini. My mother not only won't try any of my dishes, she refuses to tell any of her friends that her daughter was proudly parading around at the fair wearing a SPAM® apron and a SPAM® cap on her head.

"You know, Mother," I said dryly, "you've never even tasted it, yet you hate it. You have a prejudice against SPAM® products."

"Hilde Higgins, there is nothing wrong with being prejudiced," she said sharply. Her friends at the table next to us gasped and stared at my mother like she'd just bitten the head off a bat. "Against SPAM®!" she said, frowning at them.

In an attempt to change the subject and give our neighbors a chance to recover their bruised sensibilities, I started recounting additional details of my disastrous morning. After a while, when my mother's facial tone had recovered its normal tint, I noticed that she actually appeared to be listening. With that small amount of encouragement, I talked so much I forgot to finish my salad. I finally concluded my sad story. "So what do you think?" I asked, a little out of breath. Before she could answer, her beeper went off. Well, that was par for the course.

"I've got to go, Hilde," she said, delicately spearing the last piece of her salmon. "But I promise you, I'll think about this. In the meantime, I wouldn't tell anyone else. If you can keep this thing quiet, perhaps you'll still be able to. . .work. Other funeral directors could get skittish if they believe you've been caught stealing." She opened her purse and took out several bills, which she slid into the leather folder that contained our check. "You stay here and finish eating." She stood up, all perfect five feet eight inches of her. She leaned over and did the *kiss kiss* thing with her mouth—not actually touching my face—and then she was gone.

Clive got back to the table only a few seconds after Mother dramatically swept out of the room, every male eye in the place locked on her. He stared toward the exit with a basset hound expression and then bent down to pick up the check holder. As he straightened up, he finally noticed me sitting at the table. He looked startled. "Do you need anything else?" he asked, as if telling me my time was up and I needed to vacate the table for someone more interesting or important.

"A little more iced tea would be nice." Since my glass had been empty for the last thirty minutes, I felt it wasn't asking too much to request a refill.

"Sure, I'll be right back," he said absentmindedly. He started to reach for my salad plate.

"Um, I'm not actually finished." I grabbed the plate with both hands, trying to wrestle it out of his grip.

"Of course. Sorry."

With that, he withdrew. There was very little chance I'd see Clive or iced tea anytime soon. His reaction didn't really offend me. It's not that I'm so horrible looking I need to be running around in a tower somewhere yelling, "The bells! The bells!" but being around my mother is like placing a rather interesting rock right next to the Hope diamond. Most people aren't going to reach for the rock.

I'd just shoved a large forkful of chicken salad into my mouth when a very nice-looking man stepped up to the table.

"Aren't you Hilde Higgins?" he asked, smiling.

My answer was something like: "Mmmm mumba hibbe." I attempted to swallow my food so quickly I had to grab my mother's glass of ice water to keep from choking.

The stranger seemed amused by my distress. He sat down at the table so he could enjoy my near-death experience close up. "You don't remember me, do you?"

I shook my head. "I'm sorry," I croaked, hoping I didn't sound like Marlon Brando in *The Godfather.* "You do look familiar."

"I'm Adam. Adam Sawyer."

I almost strangled myself all over again. Adam Sawyer? The Adam Sawyer who'd moved next door to me when I was six? The Adam Sawyer who'd goaded me into eating worms? The same Adam Sawyer who saw me naked when I was seven? I said the only thing my horrified brain could come up with at that moment. "Why in heaven's name are *you* here?"

He laughed. "Well, I'm happy to see you, too. It's been a long time. I wouldn't have known it was you if it hadn't been for your mother. She looks exactly the same."

I swallowed another mouthful of water, pushing back a remark about what plastic surgery can do. I was beginning to breathe normally again, but to be honest, I wasn't too happy about running into my old childhood friend. We'd moved away after my parents' divorce when I was thirteen. That was almost ten years ago. The embarrassment of having to shower together outside after we'd gotten out of the swimming pool still resonated in my memory. I'd never seen a naked boy until that day. Let's just say I was somewhat horrified by the experience and let it go at that.

I set the glass down and flashed him my most insincere smile. "It has been a long time. What have you been doing with yourself, Adam?"

He traced an invisible pattern on the tablecloth while studying me with an expression I couldn't interpret. "Oh, not much. I'm a stockbroker with a firm here in town. And what do you do?"

I could feel my smile widen. This would put an end to this rather uncomfortable reunion. But for just a fleeting moment, I had a real twinge of regret. Adam's rather longish, dark chocolate brown hair framed a face that was almost fashion magazine handsome. Except for his nose. It was what used to be called a "Roman nose." Slightly hooked, with a bump at the bridge. It should have taken away from his looks, but somehow it didn't. It just made him more appealing.

"I. . .I'm a hairstylist," I said, not feeling quite as jubilant to turn him off as I had just a few seconds earlier. I stirred up my nerve. "For funeral homes." He looked puzzled. "I fix dead people's hair." I spit the last sentence out in an attempt to put a quick end to our brief meeting. Most people received that news as if I'd just said "I see dead people."

But my former swimming buddy threw me a curveball I didn't expect.

"Hilde Higgins, you are still the most interesting person I've ever known." His laugh was warm and genuine. Either he was getting ready to ask me for a loan or he'd been released way too early from a mental institution or he had just become the man of my dreams.

We spent the next hour reminiscing about our childhood adventures. He brought up a lot of funny things I'd forgotten over the years. Obviously the pool situation had become my traumatic focal point, driving out lots of other good memories. Could have something to do with worm poisoning—I wasn't entirely certain.

But for a little while, everything was right with the world. I wasn't basking in my mother's shadow, Clive actually brought me another glass of tea, and I forgot all about Mabel Winnemaker.

My euphoria was going to be short lived, however. Reality was waiting right around the corner.

CHAPTER FOUR

After lunch I drove home to Eden. Not the garden—the town. Eden, Kansas, is so small, most Kansans will tell you it doesn't exist. In fact, if my mail isn't addressed "Wichita," it is usually marked RETURN TO SENDER—proving that even the post office isn't certain Eden is a real place. It's located just outside of Wichita. Actually, there are two Edens, besides the original. The other one is in Atchison County. Compared to my Eden, it's a booming metropolis of almost four hundred and fifty people. My hometown consists of a few farms, a used bookstore, an antique shop, and a large, Victorian home converted into a boardinghouse. That's where I live. On the top floor in a room that was actually part of the attic until it was converted into an apartment.

My mother hates climbing the stairs to my little apartment, so she doesn't visit often. She also thinks I live in squalor. It's true the house could use a little updating, but I adore it. My room has an old iron bed that creaks comfortably when I turn over in the night. There is a small but cozy kitchen with a nook in the corner where I eat my meals, a big walk-in closet that has a lace curtain instead of a door, and a comfortable overstuffed chair covered in gold and purple paisley fabric with a matching ottoman. The chair is perfect for reading the latest mystery novel uncovered at Ida Mae Washington's bookstore, which is just about two blocks east of the boardinghouse. Next to my chair is an antique brass floor lamp I bought at Bashevis Antiques, which sits across the street. Since the only other light in the room is from a low-wattage bulb in the antiquated light fixture on the ceiling, my lamp is the only hope I have of being able to read after dark. But I'm not complaining. In fact, it creates a special ambience perfect for mysteries. On my bed is my grandmother's quilt. Her picture sits on my oak dresser. I still miss her. She passed away several years ago. She and I understood each other. My mother never understood either one of us.

My apartment has large windows that face the front of the house. They allow me to look out on fields that stretch all around our nearly invisible town. Sitting in my window seat in the late afternoon while I watch the sun slowly slip out of sight behind a fiery sky is one of my favorite things to do. A talented songwriter said it best when he described a Kansas sunset looking as though the horizon is in flames. Our red and gold evening skies are something to behold. I spend time praying and thanking God for His infinite love and blessings as I watch His magnificent handiwork colorfully splashed against the darkening easel of night.

Every floor of the house has a bathroom off the hall. Since I'm the only one on the top floor, it's like I have my own bathroom. Unfortunately, when the facilities on another floor are occupied, other tenants will come upstairs and use mine. I try to tell myself that the bathroom is for everyone, but I have to admit that it puts my nose out of joint when I find that someone else has trespassed in my upstairs domain. Last year, the man who lived below me used my bathroom frequently. In fact, he used my shampoo, my soap, and my toothpaste on more than one occasion. I suspect he may have even used my toothbrush. I finally put all my toiletries in a box, and I carry them into the bathroom with me when I need to use them. Thankfully, he finally moved out. My landlady, Arabella Hudson, told me that someone came looking for him. Something about back child support. I wasn't surprised. Anyone who would use someone else's toothbrush is probably capable of anything.

Altogether there are five of us living in the house. The second floor accommodates two residents. One is Miss Minnie Abercrombie, a widow who is a longtime friend of Mrs. Hudson's. Minnie is kind of a busybody but a well-meaning person. She and her brother owned a little diner in Nebraska before he passed away. Sometimes she and Mrs. Hudson cook big dinners and invite all the residents. Although most of the time I'd rather spend my evenings alone, I do look forward to our occasional group meals. For a little while, I feel like I'm part of a family.

A man named Isaiah Sims lives in the other apartment on the second floor. He moved in after the toothbrush borrower moved out. He's a quiet man who keeps to himself. Most days he leaves his apartment and goes somewhere. Mrs. Hudson and Minnie have tried to find out where, but so far they haven't discovered anything useful. Mrs. Hudson is a nice woman, but she likes to know everything she can about her tenants. Mr. Sims's ability to keep his business to himself doesn't sit well with her. I've spoken to him more than once, and although he's polite, he doesn't talk much. He's joined us for dinner a couple of times, but he usually leaves after we eat and before conversation really begins. Of course, most of our *conversations* are just Mrs. Hudson and Minnie going on and on about something. The rest of us are there to listen, it seems. I tried to talk about my work once, but Mrs. Hudson informed me nicely that such talk wasn't really appropriate at the table. She and my mother both have a problem with connecting death and dinner.

Mrs. Hudson's nephew, Derek, lives in the basement. He's a musician. I get the feeling he doesn't pay rent. He's supposed to take care of the yard and do odd jobs around the property. I suspect it's in exchange for a place to live. He seems okay, but I worry sometimes that he takes advantage of Mrs. Hudson. She seems to do most of the work while Derek goes off with his friends or stays downstairs. For the most part we ignore each other. I used to catch him staring at me, but he doesn't do it as much now. Not since Mrs. Hudson told him what I do for a living. I've discovered that there are a lot of people who aren't comfortable thinking about their own mortality.

As I pulled into the parking area on the side of the house, I saw Derek shoveling snow off the main sidewalk that leads to the front door. I chose to enter the side door so I wouldn't have to walk right past him. Mrs. Hudson and Minnie were at their usual places at the kitchen table, drinking tea and eating cookies. As I opened the door, I heard Minnie say, "Why, Arabella. I hate to think that someone living in this house can't be trusted. What are you going to do?"

When I stepped into the warm kitchen, both women stared at me like I was the Grim Reaper and had come to take them away. Minnie actually let out a small scream, which made me jump. This funny noise I make when I'm scared sneaked past my lips before I could suck it back in. I don't know how to describe it except to say that it sounds something like a cross between a squeak and a hiccup. But louder.

"Hilde Higgins! Why in the world are you sneaking up on us?" Mrs. Hudson's face was flushed, and her hands made little waving motions as if she were shooing away flies. "You just about scared us to death!"

I picked up my satchel, which I'd dropped when Minnie shrieked. "I—I wasn't sneaking up on you," I said, my voice quaking a little. "I just got home and decided to use the side door. I didn't realize it would frighten you. Sorry."

Mrs. Hudson shook her head, and her color returned to

normal. "Of course you didn't mean to scare us, dearie. I wasn't expecting anyone to walk in the side door. You usually come in the front."

"I know. I'll use the front door next time."

"That might be best," Mrs. Hudson said with a smile. "I just mixed up a lovely tea. Let me get you some to take upstairs. Hot tea is such a nice thing on a cold day like this, isn't it?"

While I stood there with a sappy smile plastered on my face, she scooped two big spoonfuls of her newest mixture into a plastic bag. Then she handed it to me. Mrs. Hudson spends her spare time mixing all kinds of ingredients into the stinkiest concoctions known to man. They are completely undrinkable—well, to me anyway. Minnie seems to enjoy them, but she told me not long after she moved in that her new medication affects her sense of taste. I believe her. I tried once to tell Mrs. Hudson that I didn't drink tea, but the stricken look on her face made me feel bad. After tasting the first few offerings, I decided it was in my best interests to dispose of Mrs. Hudson's little bags as soon as she gives them to me. However, I don't want her to see them in my trash can, so I usually put them in my satchel and throw them away when I'm out. A few months ago, an embalmer at a funeral home in Rose Hill, a small town a few miles from Wichita, plucked up one of the plastic bags and asked what it was. I told him. When he sniffed it, he informed me with a grimace that he used chemicals that smelled better. He didn't smile. I think he was absolutely serious.

"Here you go, sweetie," she said, handing it to me. "I blended orange pekoe with sassafras, mint, and one of my secret ingredients."

I'm pretty sure it's her "secret ingredients" that turn her tea into something not fit for human consumption. A few months ago I asked her to reveal a particular additive that smells like socks that haven't been washed for a year or so, but she declined to answer. She flashed me a coquettish smile and said, "Now, Hilde, if I tell you everything that's in my tea, it won't be as special, will it?"

I'd wanted to tell her that if I knew it was harmless, I might not have nightmares about being forced to drink her tea in an orange cup served by a clown—but I'm fairly certain that would offend her.

I was on my way upstairs when Mrs. Hudson called out, "Hilde dear, are you going out again by any chance?"

I intended to call Paula to see if we could get together for dinner. Hopefully she'd gathered some information that would help me to save my means of support—and my reputation. But even if she couldn't meet me, I had to go out anyway. My little refrigerator was bare, and I was low on fish food. We aren't allowed pets in the boardinghouse, although Mrs. Hudson has an old tabby cat that thinks it owns the place. I have a goldfish named Sherlock, which Mrs. Hudson approves of because "it's not actually a pet." But believe it or not, that silly fish is very good company. When I talk to him, he swims up to the side of the bowl and looks at me as if he's listening intently.

"I have a few errands to run," I answered as I stepped back into the kitchen. "Is there something I can do for you?"

Mrs. Hudson shuffled through some envelopes on the table. She pulled out a rather large packet and handed it to me. "The mailman delivered this here instead of to Mr. Bashevis. Do you mind dropping it off at his place when you leave?"

I did mind. Although I'd bought my lamp from Mr. Bashevis, I was not comfortable around him. Customer service isn't one of his strong points. When I'd gone to his shop to buy my lamp, I felt like an intruder. I'd made my purchase and hurried out of his store as quickly as I could. I've never been back.

I nodded and reached out my hand even though I wanted to tell Mrs. Hudson that a walk across the street wouldn't hurt her any. She and Minnie spent most of their time sitting around eating cookies and drinking stinky tea. It's not having a good effect on their waistlines. My mother would have said it, but I just smiled and said, "Sure, I'll take it by."

When I got upstairs, I put my satchel away and said hello to Sherlock. Then I called Paula. Unfortunately she had plans and asked if we could meet for lunch tomorrow. I checked my book and found that I had an appointment at Fletcher Mortuary at nine but nothing the rest of the day. We made arrangements to meet at one o'clock. Before we hung up, I brought her up to date on the diamond ring fiasco.

"Are you serious, Hilde? Something really fishy is going on at that place."

If I could have reached through the phone and hugged her, I would have. She immediately took my side. Not like my mother, who wondered if I was so addle brained I could have "accidentally picked the ring up." Or allowed it to "fall into your purse by mistake."

She assured me that she hadn't heard anything about the incident. "I think you should go to Fletcher's tomorrow and act like nothing's happened. Maybe Mr. Druther wasn't serious when he said he was going to blackball you."

"Well, he certainly looked serious. It's sure going to be hard to show up tomorrow not knowing whether or not the people at Fletcher's think I'm a kleptomaniac."

"Mark Fletcher's a good guy. If you have any problems, ask to speak to him. I think he'll listen to the truth."

"I hope you're right."

"You should probably get those pictures printed right away," Paula said. "If you have any chance of proving that the woman at Druther's isn't this Mabel person, you'll need them."

"Okay, I'll get it done tonight."

"Great, Hilde. See you tomorrow."

I hung up the phone and wondered about what she'd said about Mark Fletcher. Many of my clients, including Mark, had worked with me for a while. Who would they believe?

Me or Ron Druther?

I really wanted to stay in tonight. It certainly hadn't been a banner day in the world of Hildegard Higgins. But I'd promised Mrs. Hudson I'd take Mr. Bashevis's package to him, and I still needed to go to the store. I changed into a pair of jeans and a chambray work shirt and replaced my heels with a pair of brown leather Doc Martens. Then I pulled on my old black leather coat. I needed a new coat, and I knew it. My mother had given me one last Christmas. It hung unused in my closet—a dark brown suede with a thick wool lining. It was next to about four or five other outfits my mother bought for me. All of them nice. None of them my style. My mother never gave up trying to turn me into her version of who her daughter should be. I'd decided after moving out of her house at eighteen that I now had the right to be the person *I* wanted to be. I've been at it almost five years now, and I can't say either one of us has budged much.

I said good-bye to Sherlock by putting my face near his bowl and whispering to him. He swam up next to me, turned sideways, and waggled his side fin at me. I haven't told anyone that my goldfish waves at me. It sounds crazy. I waved back, blew him a kiss, and then grabbed my purse and the package for Mr. Bashevis. Remembering Paula's admonishment to get the pictures printed, I put my purse down and pulled my satchel out of the closet. All my supplies were there—except for the camera. Perhaps in my rush to leave Druther's I'd stuck it in my purse. I pushed the satchel back into the closet and rifled through my purse. It wasn't there. Had I accidentally left it at Druther's? Just to be sure, I searched both bags again. Nothing. Maybe it had fallen out in the car.

I hurried downstairs, this time leaving by the front door. Derek was still shoveling snow so I said hello. He didn't say anything, but I could feel his eyes on me. Derek's not a bad-looking guy. In fact, if we didn't live in the same house, I'd think he was pretty good-looking. He has thick blond hair, and his eyes are the color of the irises that grew in my grandmother's garden—deep blue with a touch of violet. The first time I saw him was not long after he moved in. It was summer, and he was weeding Mrs. Hudson's flower garden. It was hot, and he'd taken off his shirt. When I came out the back door, I'd startled him as much or more than he'd surprised me. For a few seconds I had a tough time catching my breath. I tried to convince myself it was the heat, but I knew better.

Before I got into my car, I looked in the back where I'd loaded up my satchel. Nothing. I even searched the backseat. No camera. Either I'd left it at Druther's, or someone had taken it when they'd planted Mabel's ring on me. Was this more proof that something weird was going on?

Although I could have walked across the street to Mr. Bashevis's place, I got in my car and drove. I couldn't stand the idea of Derek watching me walk across the street and back. I pulled up in front of the run-down building. Finding a parking place wasn't difficult since mine was the only car on the street except for Mr. Bashevis's old Ford truck.

Most of the paint had peeled off the building long ago, and the sign, BASHEVIS ANTIQUES, hung crookedly over the door. One good gust of wind would bring it down. Honestly, the place looked totally abandoned. In fact, more than once Mrs. Hudson and Minnie had worried that Mr. Bashevis was lying dead on the floor inside his store because he hadn't been seen in days. Mrs. Hudson checks on him every few weeks, but each time she comes huffing back, declaring "It's the last time I ever look to see if that crabby old man is still breathing!" Then a few weeks later she stomps back across the street and knocks on his door again. I was pretty sure that since she'd made her "is he alive or dead trek" about two weeks earlier, I was the designated irritant this time. Of course, I was actually bringing him his mail—and not just sticking my nose in his business. Maybe I'd get a better reception than Mrs. Hudson. I looked at the package that had been delivered by mistake. It was an odd thing for a man like Mr. Bashevis to be receiving. From someplace in the Ukraine. The return address was strange, too. The name and address of a hotel. No person's name. And Mr. Bashevis's last name was misspelled. At least I discovered that his first name isn't actually *Mr.* It's Gabriel. I wondered if anyone ever called him Gabe. Probably not.

I got out of the car and made my way to the front door. There were no footprints in the snow except mine. Suddenly the idea of finding Mr. Bashevis dead inside his store seemed a little more likely. A cold trickle of fear ran up from my toes and jumped into my brain. I see dead people almost every day, but they're *prepared* for me. The idea of finding a dead person who is just *dead*. . .well, that's a whole nother thing.

I put my hand on the front doorknob and pushed. It creaked open, and I went inside. I recognized the same musty smell from my first visit. The only real light in the room came from an ancient lamp on a table near the stairs. I was pretty sure Mr. Bashevis lived upstairs since there was a sign that read PRIVATE—KEEP OUT posted on the wall near the staircase. I wasn't sure just who the sign was for. It wasn't like the place was packed with people who might accidentally wander into the old man's private sanctuary.

"Mr. Bashevis?" I called out tentatively. I cleared my throat and tried again. "Mr. Bashevis? It's Hilde Higgins from across the street. I–I've brought your mail." There was no response. I glanced around the cluttered room. A little sunlight filtered in through cracks in the shades that covered each window. Not enough to help me see much—just enough to cast an eerie glow on some of the strange artifacts gathering dust. Even though I'd been here before, I hadn't stayed long enough to look around. An aged cigar-store Indian glared menacingly at me. There were shelves full of pottery and glass. I recognized some carnival and milk glass pieces. And a pot that looked like Roseville. I know a little about antiques and collectibles because my mother frequently buys glass and stoneware to decorate her home.

In the far corner a large, stuffed bear stood with a snarl

on his face, his claws outstretched. Hanging from one paw was a woman's beaded purse with what appeared to be an image of the Eiffel Tower. On the other paw were several ladies' scarves. The poor bear looked like some kind of giant, scary salesperson. I'm not sure whether it was that ridiculous image or just nerves, but a giggle forced its way through my clenched teeth.

"Would you like to share the joke, or is it private?"

The gruff male voice startled me, and I bit my tongue. The next sound I made wasn't a laugh—it was closer to a screech of pain. I turned around to see Mr. Bashevis glaring at me.

"Are you in the habit of breaking into people's homes and making unusual noises?" he asked, his thick eyebrows locked together like two battling caterpillars.

"I thought this was a business." My words sounded thick and unclear. I tried to ignore my injured tongue. "Perhaps you need to remove the sign outside if you don't want customers." My irritation was clearer than my speech.

"I see." The old man stood, staring at me, his arms folded across his chest. "So you've come here to buy something? Perhaps a knickknack to go with the lamp you purchased a couple of months ago? What kind of windfall can I expect this time? Perhaps an old magazine for two dollars? Or better yet, I have some lace doilies for fifty cents. Why don't you go all out this time?"

The indignity of biting my tongue and being ridiculed by

someone I was doing a favor for got the best of me. I have an embarrassing habit of crying when I'm mad. And I was about as angry as I could get.

"I—I'm sorry I took the time to come over here and bring this to you." I stomped over to where he stood and thrust the package toward him, wiping my drippy eyes with my sleeve. "I have a life, you know. I only did this to—to help you!" I was trying to conjure up a few more choice words to make him feel contrite for his actions when he stumbled backward and almost fell over. His eyes were glued on the packet in his hands, and almost all the color had drained completely out of his face.

I forgot about being upset with him. I also forgot about my damaged tongue. I grabbed his arm and steadied him. "I think you need to sit down, Mr. Bashevis," I said gently. I glanced around the room. There was a chair near the counter where the cash register sat. I guided him over and helped him into it. He didn't say a word; he just stared at the envelope.

"Can I get you a glass of water?"

He nodded slowly. "Please," he whispered. "Upstairs. In the kitchen."

I left him sitting there and ran up the stairs. The hallway opened up into a large living room. If I hadn't been so worried about the elderly man downstairs, I would have been forced to stand in the middle of the room for a few minutes and gawk. The shabby environment in the shop gave way to surprising elegance. Gleaming wood floors, a large Oriental rug, brown leather furniture, and artwork that certainly didn't look like anything sold at Bashevis Antiques. A fire crackled in the fireplace, and on a small table next to a beautiful leather chair, tea steeped in a decorative ceramic pot. And it didn't smell the least bit stinky. I forced my feet to move and passed through the living room and into a kitchen that was just as astonishing as the rest of the apartment. Functional, state-of-the-art, with gleaming stainless steel appliances. I fumbled around in the cabinets until I located the glasses. I started to pour water from the tap, but then I noticed a water dispenser in the door of the massive refrigerator and used that instead. After a final glance around, I rushed down the stairs with the water.

Mr. Bashevis still sat in the chair where I'd left him, but now he was holding a pill bottle. When he saw me, he quickly slipped the bottle back into his pocket, but not before I noticed the small white pill in his hand. I gave him the water, and he drank it slowly. For some reason it seemed like he didn't want me to see him take the pill he'd palmed, so I made a point of turning around and looking out the window.

"It's starting to snow again," I said. "Hopefully the streets won't get too bad."

There was no response. I turned around. The pill was no longer in his hand, and the glass was empty.

"Can I get you more water?" I asked.

He shook his head slowly. His gnarled fingers held the

glass so tightly they were white. I was afraid he would break it so I reached out for it. He stared at my outstretched hand for a moment then released his hold, and I took it from him. I set it on the counter next to the cash register. The old man didn't say anything, just gazed down at his lap.

"Are you okay, Mr. Bashevis? Is there something else I can do for you?"

"No. No, thank you Miss. . .Miss. . ."

"It's Higgins. But please call me Hilde."

"A cross between the saint and the flower girl," he mumbled. He looked up at me. "You see, there is a famous German abbess who. . ."

"I know," I said, interrupting him. "Hildegard of Bingen. I'm named after her."

His thick eyebrows arched in surprise. "How interesting. Not many people know about her."

"It gets worse. My middle name is Bernadette. My mother was going through a fascination with saints when she was pregnant with me."

For the first time since I'd known Mr. Bashevis, he smiled. The change in his face surprised me. He was actually quite attractive for a man his age. I could tell that in his younger years he was probably very handsome. I would have never acquainted Mr. Bashevis with the word *handsome* until that moment. I found the thought compelling and slightly disturbing. I was trying to remember the last time I'd had a date when he interrupted my thoughts.

"I want to thank you for your assistance, Miss. . .Hilde," he said, rising slowly from his chair. "I have no idea what came over me. Old age does strange things to the body." He reached out and touched my arm. "I would also like to ask your forgiveness for speaking to you so harshly." He sighed and put his hand down. "I guess I've spent so much time alone I've forgotten how to treat people. I am truly repentant for my behavior. I hope you can find it in your heart to forgive me and extend me another chance."

When he stood up, he pushed the package I'd delivered under his chair. I wasn't buying the "old age" bit. There was something about that packet that had upset him. And it was obviously a topic we weren't going to discuss. Okay by me. Although I was curious about it, I had problems of my own. I didn't have time to worry about an old man and his misdirected mail.

"It's no problem, Mr. Bashevis," I said. "I'm just glad you're okay. I really have to be going."

"Wait a minute." The old man shuffled behind the large counter and bent down. I heard him moving things around. Finally he stood up. He clutched something in his hand. "I would like you to have this." He set the object on the counter, and I stepped closer to see it. It looked like a small cage with something inside. I peered into it. A little yellow bird sat perched on a tree limb. As I was wondering just what I was going to do with a dusty toy bird in a cage, Mr. Bashevis picked it up and turned a key on the bottom. Then he put it back on the counter. The bird's head began to move back and forth, and his beak opened and closed. The most beautiful music filled the room. It was absolutely enchanting. Mr. Bashevis and I kept quiet until the song wound down.

"I love it," I said with a smile, "but I don't see how I can accept it. It must be valuable."

Mr. Bashevis shook his head and frowned. "There once was a king who refused to offer something to the Lord that didn't cost him anything," he said in a low voice. He pushed the bird toward me. "Perhaps an item shouldn't be judged by its monetary value. It's the thought behind it that counts. Besides, you should not look a gift horse in the mouth, young lady." He slapped his hands together as if trying to brush the dust off them. "It's been sitting in this shop for a long, long time. I put it under the counter because I'd given up trying to sell it. Either you take it or it goes in the trash. Your choice."

I stared at the small yellow bird that seemed to be looking back at me. I couldn't allow anything so wonderful to be thrown away. Besides, if I didn't take it, the old man might come up with another worn-out platitude. I couldn't risk it. "Thank you, Mr. Bashevis. I love it. I promise to take very good care of it."

"You may do whatever you wish with it," he said dismissively. He reached for a plastic bag and wrapped the bird up in it. "Thank you for bringing me my mail. And thank you for helping me today. I appreciate it."

He held out the bag, and I took it. I turned to leave and then stopped. Gabriel Bashevis had sad eyes, and it bothered me. "Mr. Bashevis," I said, turning around and looking at him. "I wonder if you would consider having dinner with me tonight. I could pick up something and bring it over, say around six thirty?"

He hesitated and looked down at the floor. I was sure I'd made a mistake. Not that it mattered. I'd never have to face him again if I didn't want to. I was just about ready to make my getaway when he surprised me.

"I could make something," he said quietly.

Was the old man agreeing to eat with me? I could hardly believe it. "You need to rest. Why don't you let me take care of it? Maybe next time you could cook." *Next time?* Now I'd not only invited myself over for dinner, I'd created a future social occasion. Maybe I could just run for the door and pretend this never happened. I heard once that if you move fast enough, you can go back in time. . . .

He raised one eyebrow and looked at me suspiciously. "What kind of food would you bring?"

Although I knew most of the restaurants on the east side of Wichita, my mind was blank. Then I remembered a great carryout that had the best sandwiches in town. "Barn'rds makes great roast beef sandwiches. They also have a yummy horseradish sauce. Or if you'd rather have something else. . ."

He waved his hand at me. "No, no. That sounds very good. Thank you, Miss Higgins."

"Hilde," I reminded him again.

"Then you must call me Gabe. Mr. Bashevis is my father."

Gabe. There it was. This was going to be difficult. "Thank you, G–Gabe. I'll be back by six thirty."

"That will be fine."

He turned around and began fiddling with something behind him. I took his actions as a sign that it was time for me to go. I picked up the package with the bird music box and hurried to the door. When I pulled it open, it squeaked loudly. Probably from lack of use. Before I went outside, I said loudly enough for him to hear, "By the way. That was David. The king who wouldn't offer a sacrifice that didn't cost him anything." Without waiting for a response, I closed the door behind me and left.

CHAPTER FIVE

Mr. Bashevis's gift to me may or may not have cost him something, but as I waited in the drive-through at Barn'rds, I began to count the cost of the gift I'd extended to him. Me. I really wasn't too excited to be spending the evening with a grouchy old man I had nothing in common with. I was next in line when my cell phone rang. I put my car in PARK and flipped my phone open, hoping it wasn't Fletcher's calling to cancel my appointment in the morning.

"Hello?"

"Hilde? Is that you?"

It was a male voice I didn't recognize at first. Then I realized who it was. Adam.

"Yes. Yes, it's me."

"It's Adam. Adam Sawyer."

Like I knew another Adam. I'd forgotten I'd given him my number. Funny to forget something like that. I probably blocked it in case he never called. The woman in front of me took her food and started to leave.

"Adam, can you hold on for a minute? I'm in the drive-through, and it's my turn."

"Sure. I'll hold."

I put the phone down on the seat next to me and pulled up to the window, my hand clasping a twenty-dollar bill. The woman slid the little glass door open and stuck her hand out.

"That'll be sixteen fifty-three," she said with a smile.

In my rushed attempt to finish my transaction and get back to Adam, I released the bill a little too quickly. I watched in horror as the woman tried to grab it before it was picked up by the wind and carried somewhere above my car.

"Oh, shoot!" I tried to open my car door, but I was trapped. I was too close to the building, and the door would only open a few inches. I picked up the phone. "Adam, hang on. My money is flying around the parking lot. I'll be right back!"

I climbed over the stick shift to the other side of the car and got out. A brief chase ensued until my twenty was finally trapped under the front tire of a car parked a few yards away. I crawled under the car to retrieve it. When I slid out, I found myself looking up into the face of a man with a paper bag in his hand. His expression reminded me of the first time my mother had seen my newly colored hair.

"Is there some reason you're under my car, young lady?"

At this, the door above me opened and a woman leaned over and stared down at me. "She lost her money, Jack," she said, her mouth quivering with laughter. "It flew under our car."

He handed her the bag and held out his hand. I took it, and he pulled me to my feet. "In the future, you should be more careful," he said.

I could have mentioned that he was stating the obvious, but I didn't. I just said, "Thank you," and slunk back to my car. I could hear his wife giggling behind me.

After climbing back over the stick shift, I held out my money to the lady at the window once again. This time I held on tightly, determined not to let go until I was certain she had a tight grip on it.

"I'm sorry, honey," she said, looking apologetic, "but I can't take that."

I stared down at the bill clasped in my hand. Or should I say, the half a bill clasped in my hand. A glance toward the couple whose car I'd crawled under told me the "rest of the story," as they say. I watched while they pulled out of their parking space, the other part of my twenty escaping from under one of their tires. The wind scooted it up and danced it merrily across the parking lot right into the street.

A honk from the car behind me confirmed what I already knew. The people waiting in line were getting frustrated, and my antics were not endearing me to the hungry dinner crowd that simply wanted their roast beef sandwiches without all the entertainment.

I grabbed my purse and started digging around. There were no more twenties. I found some ones, a five, and some change. I counted it out. It came to nine dollars and twelve cents. I was about to ask the woman if she was interested in a four-year-old watch when I remembered my emergency pocket. I always try to keep a spare bill tucked away in an inside pocket of my jacket for occasions just like this. Okay, so there had never been an occasion quite like this before, but the idea was the same. I slipped my hand into the pocket and pulled out a ten. I whispered a quick "thank-you" to God. Then I counted out seventeen dollars and handed it carefully to the woman. She took it gratefully and gave me my food. I pulled away without my change. I wondered if I'd be able to return to Barn'rds without getting a different car and dying my hair. Then I remembered Adam. I almost swerved into the other lane as I grabbed the phone. Fearing for my safety and the lives of others, I turned into the parking lot at a strip mall and pulled into a parking spot.

"Adam?" I said into my phone, not actually expecting him to be there. He was. I tried to briefly explain the situation without sounding like a complete airhead.

"Hilde, you're something else. I've never known anyone like you." His statement was followed by hearty laughter.

Good thing he couldn't see through the phone. A glance in the rearview mirror revealed a red-faced woman with wet hair. The snow that had settled on my head was melting. Rivulets of water dripped into my eyes. All in all, I looked like a thoroughly drenched dog.

"I'm happy I could amuse you," I said, a little more sarcastically than I meant to.

"I'm sorry." His tone became more subdued, although I had the feeling it took him some effort. "Are you okay?"

"I'm fine. Except I'm out twenty dollars, I'm soaked, and I'm running late for a dinner date."

There were a few seconds of silence before Adam said, "Oh. Sorry. Didn't mean to keep you from a date. Anyone important?"

It was obvious the poor deranged man thought I had an actual *date* date. I started to explain about Mr. Bashevis, but then I realized that it wasn't Adam's business anyway. Why did I feel the need to go into detail? At the same time, a little voice in my head urged me to find out whether or not this relationship had a chance to become more than a reunion of two old childhood buddies.

"I'm just getting together with a friend. I really am running late, and my food's getting cold. Maybe you could call me later tonight or tomorrow?"

He cleared his throat. Was he nervous about something? Interesting.

"Actually, I was wondering if you'd like to. . .well. . . maybe get together? How about dinner tomorrow night?"

Suddenly the scene I'd caused at Barn'rds didn't seem quite so bad. "I—I guess that would be all right. What time and where?"

"What about Yen Ching out east? Seven okay?"

I was relieved to hear Adam mention one of my favorite places—a beautiful restaurant with a warm, relaxed atmosphere. They serve one of the best dishes in Wichita. Sweet and Spicy Three Ingredients. A perfect mix of chicken, beef, and huge shrimp in a sauce so delicious it makes me want to lick my plate clean. Perhaps not the right thing to do on a first date. Another great thing about Yen Ching is the staff. The friendliest in town. And no waiters named Clive. "Sounds wonderful. I'll see you there."

"Great. And Hilde?"

"Yes?" I said, trying to put my car into gear while balancing the phone.

"It's my treat, so you can leave all your flying money at home."

"Very funny."

I said good-bye, turned off my phone, and shoved it into my purse again. Then I took off for Mr. Bashevis's. A look at the clock on my dashboard told me I was only going to be a few minutes late. Hopefully the old man wasn't as strict as my mother.

I pulled in front of the old antique store and got out of the car. The door to the shop was open. I carried the bag of food inside and looked for Mr. Bashevis, but I didn't see him anywhere.

"Is that you, Hilde?" His voice drifted down from upstairs.

"Yes, it's me. Do you want me to come up there?"

"Come on."

I was glad we were eating upstairs instead of in the dusty

shop. Besides, I'd only gotten a quick glance at Mr. Bashevis's apartment. I was curious about it—and about him. I reached the top of the stairs and entered the living room. A fire crackled in the fireplace, and I smelled something yummy.

Mr. Bashevis stepped out from the kitchen. "I thought we'd eat in here if that's okay. It's a little cozier than the dining room."

The dining room? This place had a dining room? Sure enough, as I headed toward the kitchen, I noticed another room I hadn't seen before, just off the living room. It was a lovely room with a small, crystal chandelier. A beautiful table with six chairs sat in the middle. I couldn't tell for certain, but it looked like mahogany. My mother has an expensive mahogany dining room set—but this was even better than hers. A massive buffet sat against one wall. Over it hung a painting. I only caught a quick glance, but the face in the frame belonged to a gorgeous woman with red hair and sad eyes.

I turned my attention back to Mr. Bashevis, who was busy pouring something into small china teacups sitting in saucers. The cups were delicately decorated with gold flowers against a cobalt blue background. Gabriel Bashevis was certainly turning out to be an enigma. His clothes appeared to be at least twenty years old, and his hair always seemed to need a good combing. That persona didn't jive with the way he lived. How in the world could he afford all this? I'd never seen customers in his shop. And why was the store such a mess? It's obvious the man knew how to decorate. And even more important—how to clean.

The aroma coming from the pot in Mr. Bashevis's hand told me that I probably didn't need to worry about stinky tea. It smelled wonderful.

"It's a Darjeeling blend," Mr. Bashevis said, noticing my interest. "It's called builder's tea. Strong enough to stand a spoon up in." He finished pouring and then motioned to one of the chairs at the kitchen table. The set was wood with wicker accents, and the chairs had high backs and padded seats with a lovely floral pattern. The wicker accents matched the scrolled carved wood pattern that decorated the sides of the table. A round piece of glass protected the cherry wood top. The set wasn't new, but it was well taken care of—and breathtaking. A glance around the kitchen confirmed what I'd noticed earlier. This kitchen was not only high tech it was charming. Compared to the stainless steel appliances in this kitchen, my ancient refrigerator and range with only one working burner looked like dog meat next to prime rib. I had no idea how much a monster-size refrigerator with an ice and water dispenser in the door costs, but I was pretty sure I wouldn't be having one delivered to my place anytime soon. Mr. Bashevis opened one of its huge doors and took out a jar of pickles. The fridge was pretty well stocked.

"I think that's it." Mr. Bashevis set the pickles on the table. "Why don't you get our sandwiches out while I wash my hands?"

He turned toward the sink, and I started pulling sandwiches and fries out of the bag. They looked a little funny on gleaming white china plates next to the froufrou teacups, but I wasn't worried about how they were going to taste. I tried to make the sandwiches and fries look as appetizing as possible. By the time Mr. Bashevis finished his hand washing, we were ready to eat. I was surprised when he held my chair out for me.

"Do you mind if I pray over our food?" he asked when we were both seated.

"That would be nice." I wondered if he wanted to offer thanks or seek protection. I needn't have worried. He simply thanked God for the meal and for bringing him such "charming company."

I thanked him and picked up the little plastic cup that held Barn'rds's wonderful horseradish sauce. I pulled up the top bun on my sandwich and poured the creamy mixture on the succulent roast beef. Then I took a big bite and used my chewing time to study my host. His manners were impeccable—cloth napkin on his lap, pinkie extended when he sipped his tea. He even cut his sandwich in half before eating it. I could usually figure people out after being around them for a little while. But understanding Gabriel Bashevis was a challenge.

I started to take a sip of the tea he'd poured for me, but he stopped me. "This tea needs some sugar and milk. May I?"

I said yes and watched while he tweaked my tea. When

he finished, I took a sip. Strong, with a robust flavor, it really complemented the roast beef. I nodded at him. "It's delicious."

He cleared his throat and smiled at me. "Mrs. Hudson told me a little bit about your job one day when she wandered over to see if I'd kicked the bucket. Very interesting. Tell me how you ended up as a mortuary beautician."

I explained that I wasn't actually a mortuary beautician, since they handle much more than just hair. Between bites I told him the story of how I'd found my unusual profession. He listened intently and seemed genuinely interested. Little by little I started to feel more relaxed. The good food and the wonderful tea helped push away the rotten morning I'd had. Then, somehow, without making a conscious decision to do it, I found myself telling the old man about Mabel Winnemaker and the catastrophic events of the day.

I realized I was sharing very personal information, but there was something about Mr. Bashevis's manner and his questions that seemed to pull things out of me. Part of my mind was yelling at my mouth to shut up while some other section of my brain pushed the torrent of words out between lips that were happy to flap away. It was very strange and quite disconcerting. Finally, after I blathered out everything I could think of, I stopped. I stared wide-eyed at this man I barely knew. Why in the world had I shared my very private trials with such aplomb?

"You're being framed," he said, picking up his cup and

taking a sip. He put it down and looked at me through narrowed eyes. "Finding out the truth won't be easy, but it can be done. Someone at Druther's must know that Mabel is missing. I suspect they also know why."

"But how do I find out what happened to her?"

He leaned back in his chair and crossed his arms. "You shouldn't have to. As soon as the family views the body, the jig will be up, as they say."

"I hope so. But the grandson won't be back in time for the funeral, and the nephew has requested a closed casket. If he doesn't change his mind. . ."

"Then you change it for him. Contact him and tell him your concerns. Urge him to check. Once he realizes that the woman in the casket isn't his aunt, the whole problem will be dumped back in the mortuary's lap."

"But what if he doesn't believe me? What if Ron Druther tells him I'm some kind of nut who tried to steal his aunt's jewelry? And what if. . ."

"Stop!" The tone in his voice pulled me up short. "Spending your time on the what-if road is a certain trip to nowhere. Find out how to contact this man. When the obituary comes out, you'll see his name. It should be fairly easy to find him after that. I imagine a quick look at the phone book might also help. How many Winnemakers could there be?"

"I don't know, but the grandson's name is William Winnemaker. The nephew's name is Alfred. William lives in Japan, and Alfred's address is 826 N. Livingston in Wichita.

I also have his phone number."

Mr. Bashevis's eyebrows shot up. "How did you come by all this information?"

I shrugged. "I saw Mabel's file while I was at Druther's."

He frowned at me. "Those are pretty specific details. How long did you look at that file?"

"A few seconds. I have. . ."

"A photographic memory," he said, interrupting me.

I nodded. "It comes in handy sometimes."

"Yes, I imagine it does." He grunted and stared at me. I wondered if he was thinking about the package I'd delivered to him earlier. I could remember the return address clearly, as well as the person it was delivered to. Gabriel Bastian. Not Bashevis. It didn't mean anything to me and was certainly nothing for him to worry about. I got mail all the time with either my first or last name misspelled. One of my magazine subscriptions had never gotten it right, even after several attempts to correct it. I was almost used to being referred to as *Hilly Hickens*.

He cleared his throat and continued. "The theft charge against you is obviously connected to this woman's disappearance. When she's found, however, there might still be questions about the diamond ring. You need as much information as you can obtain in case one problem doesn't solve the other—and in case the nephew decides not to view the body. To get the kind of answers you want, you must contact an employee at the funeral home. Believe me, someone there has information that should help you. Although you might not get one person to tell you everything you need to know, there may be someone else who holds another piece of the puzzle. Many times you have to put all the bits and pieces together to form that final picture. It means turning over every rock. You never know when something might crawl out."

"But I can't even enter the building. Ron told me not to ever come back. He's probably already called all the other funeral homes in town. I'm just waiting for a phone call cancelling my appointment tomorrow."

"Even that will tell you something."

I frowned at him. "What do you mean?"

"If Mr. Druther *doesn't* call the other directors, you have to ask yourself, why? Is it because he's in on it? Or does he believe you? And if he believes you, why didn't he help you?" He shook his head slowly. "Everything everyone does now is important, Hilde. You've got to pay careful attention."

I drained the last drop of tea from my cup. I could hear the winter wind howling outside, but the kitchen was warm and inviting. "But if Ron doesn't spread the alarm, maybe I should leave well enough alone. I'd only lose the Druther account. I can live with that."

He smiled slowly. "I haven't known you long, but I doubt seriously if you can walk away now. You're a bright and curious young lady. You want to know what's going on." He leaned back in his chair, his eyes locked on my face. "Hilde,

Ron Druther has information that can hurt you. True or not, if you walk away and leave that power in his hands, it can hang over you the rest of your life." He sighed and shook his head. "Trust me, it isn't the way to live." He leaned forward, his gaze direct and a little challenging. "Besides, what about Mabel?"

Mabel's picture, with her kind eyes and that goofy dog, popped into my mind. What about Mabel? I'd ventured into the world of funeral homes and dead bodies because I'd felt called to it. Could I walk away from her? And could I walk away from Ron Druther's threats? Mr. Bashevis was right. I had to try to get my reputation back and bring Mabel's life to a more satisfying conclusion.

I returned his penetrating stare with one of my own. "Mr. Bashevis, I can't just waltz into Druther's and start questioning people."

He frowned. "I thought you were going to call me Gabe."

"I'm sorry. You're right, Gabe."

He grinned and picked up his teacup. "Like I said, you need a mole. Someone on the inside to help you get what you need."

I raised my eyebrows. "A *mole*? What are you, an ex-spy or something?"

The smile on his face vanished like smoke in the wind. "Don't be ridiculous, Hilde." He set his cup on his saucer. It rattled into place. "If you don't want my help. . ."

"I—I do. Sorry. I was just kidding." Why had he reacted so severely to my little joke? I wondered about the curious old man sitting across from me. About his strange package, his ability to get me to spill my guts, all the advice about how to solve puzzles. Just who was Gabriel Bashevis?

He sighed and waved his hand dismissively. "No, I'm sorry. But I am concerned that this situation might be more important than you realize. I feel you should take it very seriously."

I sighed. "Okay, so back to the mole business. There are really only two possibilities." I told him about Gwen and Eddie.

He rubbed his chin and asked a few questions about them. After I answered, he was quiet for several seconds. Finally he said, "I think you need to contact Gwen. You might get what you need from this Eddie character, but he would probably expect payback for his assistance. I don't think you're willing to pay his price."

I rolled my eyes. "Thank you. I do have my limits. Mata Hari I'm not."

He laughed. "What about Gwen?"

"We know each other, but we're not close friends. She did seem upset by what happened. How do I get her to talk to me?"

Gabe grinned. "You ask. That's always the first step."

"But what if Gwen tells Ron Druther that I want to see her?"

He raised one eyebrow and looked at me like I was simple.

And I felt like it. "Then we try something else. But if what you say about this Druther character is true, I doubt he's built up much loyalty from his staff. He sounds like the kind of man who doesn't make friends with his employees. Besides, people enjoy gossip. Gwen would probably love to talk about your circumstances. I'll bet it's the most interesting thing that's happened there in some time."

"That sounds reasonable, but I have one last question."

"What if she is involved in Mabel's disappearance? And what if she is the one who put the ring in your purse?"

I nodded.

"Then she will want to see you to find out what you know. She'll want to make certain you don't suspect her. If she's a part of the plot, you'll know it."

I frowned at him. "How could I possibly know that? I have a photographic memory—not ESP."

Gabe grunted. "Think it through, Hilde. If she's involved, she'll do everything she can to dissuade you from pursuing the matter. If she's not mixed up in it, she'll show normal curiosity—even offer to help you."

I considered this. "I see your point."

"Now *I* have a question," Gabe said. "Where was this ring? Was it on the body?"

"No. It was locked up. That's why it would have been impossible for me to steal it."

He sighed. "Hilde, that's very important. If you didn't

have access to the ring, it proves that someone from the funeral home put it in your purse."

I felt my jaw drop. "You're right. I never thought about. . ." Suddenly a picture of the room where I'd been introduced to the fake Mabel popped into my mind. Having a photographic memory is like someone suddenly shoving color pictures in front of you. I could see everything just like I was still standing there: the table, the body, the storage cabinets. . . and a set of keys lying on the counter. "Oh, shoot."

"What's the matter?" Gabe asked.

"The keys. The keys *were* there. I just remembered. If I'd wanted to, I could have opened the jewelry drawer. That must be why Ron Druther suspected me."

"Who would have left those keys lying out?"

I shook my head. "It could have been almost anyone. The staff was waiting for me to finish Mabel's hair so the jewelry could be placed."

Gabe's forehead wrinkled. "Why would a corpse have jewelry in the first place? Especially if the casket is going to be closed?"

I shrugged. "Happens all the time. Most people want to be buried wearing their wedding rings. That was probably the case with Mabel. You wouldn't believe some of the weird things I've seen in coffins."

He seemed to accept this premise, and we continued to discuss what steps I should take next. I began to wonder if

I was heading in a direction that would help me out of my predicament—or would pull me deeper into something I might not be able to get out of. That question rolled around uncomfortably in my mind for the rest of the evening.

CHAPTER ⑊⑊⑊ SIX

I showed up at Fletcher's the next morning, wondering if they were going to toss me out, but everything seemed normal. I finished my work without any complications and was gone within an hour. I still had three hours before my lunch date with Paula.

I didn't want to drive all the way back to Eden, so I decided to go to the mall and do a little Christmas shopping. Since I didn't have much money and wasn't sure if my finances would soon be drying up, I didn't buy much. But it was fun poking around and looking at all the things I didn't dare purchase.

A little before noon I decided to get a cup of coffee and sit in the food court until it was time to meet Paula. I spotted a newspaper someone had left on a table and grabbed it. A quick look through the obituaries led me to a brief entry about Mabel.

Wichita—Winnemaker, Mabel K., 87,

loving grandmother and aunt and retired
medical records clerk, died December 7th.
Service 11 a.m., Friday, Druther's Funeral
Home. Preceded in death by husband James,
daughter Margaret, sister Emmaline. Survivors:
grandson William Winnemaker, nephew Alfred
Winnemaker (Edith). This is a Druther's service.

Even though I knew I'd remember it, I tore out the obituary and stuffed it in my purse. Then I checked my watch. It was twelve fifteen. I'd learned from previous visits to Druther's that Gwen always took lunch at one o'clock because Ron insisted on having lunch at twelve on the dot. That meant she was at the funeral home, and he was most likely gone. After searching through my purse, I found my cell phone and pulled it out. As I did, a pen fell out and bounced on the floor. I leaned over and picked it up. Great. A new entry in my weird collection. It was black with silver writing on the side that read FLYING DEMON MOTORCYCLE CLUB—PHOENIX, ARIZONA. "You've got to be kidding," I said out loud. Where in the world would I have picked this up? I shook my head and put it back in my purse. I wasn't sure I wanted to contact the Flying Demons and ask them if they wanted their pen back.

I dialed Druther's number. Gwen answered on the second ring.

"Druther's Funeral Home. This is Gwen; may I help you?"

I suddenly felt nervous. Gwen had always been nice to me. Could she really believe I was capable of lying about a body and stealing jewelry from a dead person?

"Hello?" Gwen said again.

"G–Gwen, it's Hilde. Hilde Higgins. Can I talk to you a minute?"

"Hilde! I've been so worried. How are you?"

Encouraged by her positive response, I said, "I'm okay. But I'm a little concerned about my career taking a nosedive."

She sighed. "I don't know what will happen, Hilde. Ron is still pretty upset, but as far as I know, he hasn't called anyone. That doesn't mean he won't. Next Friday there's a meeting scheduled for a lot of the local directors. If he's going to say something, it will probably be then."

Today was Thursday. I had eight days to prove my innocence. Not a lot of time.

"Look Gwen, can we get together? I need to ask you a few questions. And please don't tell Mr. Druther."

She hesitated for a few seconds. I sent up a quick prayer for help. If I couldn't get some information from her, Eddie was next on the list, and I really hoped I wouldn't have to go there.

"It will have to be tonight after work. Tomorrow a friend and I are leaving town and heading someplace warm for the weekend. My intention is to exchange the frozen plains of Kansas for sunshine and palm trees. I have to stay for a viewing tonight that won't be over until seven. It will take me a couple of hours after that to get everything caught up so I can head out tomorrow. I could meet you somewhere nearby about nine. Will that work?"

I had a dinner date with Adam at seven. Would it be rude to tell him I had another appointment at nine? I had no choice. Time was of the essence. "That will be fine, Gwen. Thanks. How about coffee at the Starbucks down the street?"

She agreed, and we hung up. One thing off the list. Hopefully I could find out something from Gwen that would help the situation. I certainly didn't look forward to contacting Mabel's family for information.

I checked my watch. I had twenty minutes before I met Paula. I left the mall and drove to the café where we'd decided to have lunch. Egg Cetera is a quaint restaurant located in the Old Town district of Wichita. Creative city leaders had taken a run-down area full of old commercial buildings and turned them into lofts, restaurants, museums, theaters, shops, and businesses. Thankfully the revamped buildings still retained their "old town" charm. This part of Wichita is now alive and thriving. Even though I don't consider myself a "big city" girl, I do enjoy visiting Old Town.

I walked into the restaurant a couple of minutes before one. Polished wood floors supported cozy tables and booths with tablecloths and flowers. Golden walls were decorated with local art, and modern painted lights hung down from wooden rafters. Paula sat in a corner booth, waiting for me. She smiled and waved me over. Not that I would have missed her. Her newest hair color was stoplight red. Paula changed her hair color as often as other women change their purses.

I slid into the booth across from her. "Thanks for meeting me," I said, reaching over and patting her hand. "I really need your advice."

"You get yourself in the strangest situations, Hilde," she said, shaking her head.

She started to say something else, but the waitress interrupted her, bringing us menus and water. I watched Paula as she placed her order for a granola, yogurt, and fruit concoction. We'd attended the same high school, and even though I'd known who she was, I didn't find out until we became friends after my graduation that her bubbly, outgoing personality hid a painful home life. Unfortunately, the church her parents belong to hasn't helped. They present God the same way she sees her parents—as judgmental and distant. To Paula, He is someone she can't understand and who doesn't understand her. Two years older than I am, she already has two failed marriages behind her. About a year ago, she'd gotten entangled in some kind of new age ideas, and now she thinks she has all the answers to life. But she doesn't. In fact, she doesn't even understand the questions. I've tried to explain to her more than once that none of us can know ourselves without knowing the One who created us, but she associates everything "religious" to what she's seen in the life of her parents and the people who attend their church. I pray constantly that God will help me show her who He *really* is instead of the skewed picture she has in her mind.

I ordered the quiche Lorraine along with Egg Cetera's incredible ambrosia salad. As soon as the waitress walked away, Paula leaned forward. "So what's going on, Hilde? Anything else happen since you talked to me?"

I nodded. "My camera's gone. I've looked everywhere. Either the person who planted that ring on me took it, or I left it at Druther's. I don't know what to do."

Paula drew back, her face screwed up into a grimace. "Wow. You really need those pictures. Is there anyone at Druther's you trust enough to ask about the camera?"

I shrugged. "Maybe. I'm meeting Gwen Cox tonight. I'll check with her."

Paula took a long sip of water and then put her glass down. She drank more water than anyone I'd ever met. I was surprised she hadn't brought her own personal water bottle with her into the restaurant. But I'd have bet a year's salary, my PT Cruiser, and Sherlock that there were several bottles waiting for her in her car.

"I heard Gwen has a new honey," she said, lowering her voice as if anyone else in the restaurant cared. "Melba from Eternal Rest saw her crawling all over some guy at The Nomad the other night."

The Nomad's a coffee shop slash bar in the Delano District, an area not far from Old Town. It was frequented by the avant-garde crowd, and I'd determined after a couple of visits that it wasn't for me. I would have called it a "yuppie hangout," but I've been told that the word *yuppie* isn't "in" anymore. All in all, I usually run about five years behind what's fashionable. Except for my new hairstyle. At least I have that.

"I hope he's someone who will treat her well," I said. It was common knowledge that Gwen had made a few poor choices in the past. I never could understand why women with as much going for them as Gwen Cox and Paula picked men who treated them like last week's garbage.

"There aren't that many good men out there, Hilde," Paula said slowly. "Sometimes you just have to jump in and take your chances."

I smiled at her. "Well, as a matter of fact. . ."

Her face lit up. "Oh my goodness! Don't tell me there's actually a man in our little Hilde's life."

I briefly told her about running into Adam and our upcoming date.

"He sounds dreamy," she said with a smile. "Does he have money, too?"

"I didn't actually ask him his bank balance," I said, laughing. "All I know is that he's a stockbroker."

"Sounds like you've hooked a good one. I'll send some positive energy your way."

I wasn't sure that "positive energy" would be helpful in my relationship with Adam—and I was put off by her question about how much money he made—but I thanked her anyway. Then I changed the subject.

"So have you come up with anything that might help me out of this lovely little scrape I'm in?"

"I talked to Gus about it, and I discovered some rather interesting things."

Paula was lucky to be working for Gus Dorado. Gus and his family owned one of Wichita's premier mortuaries. Willowbrook Funeral Home was the Cadillac of funeral homes. In fact, about sixty percent of my clients came from Willowbrook. I was extremely interested in what he had to say. If I could keep his account, I would probably be able to keep my apartment and at least eat sporadically. Of course, I wouldn't be able to buy gas for my car, but I'd figure that out later.

"Well," Paula said dramatically, "you know I don't like to gossip, but Gus told me that Ron Druther is in terrible financial trouble. He wonders if your situation is connected somehow."

"How in the world would Ron Druther's financial problems be connected to losing a body?" I rubbed my fingers on my temples. I could feel the beginnings of a headache. "I doubt that he sold Mabel. I don't think he'd make much money."

"You know," Paula said, arching her eyebrows, "I've heard there are people who buy body parts. . . ."

Even though I was upset, I couldn't hold back a giggle. "You think there's a big market for old, used-up body parts from elderly women? What kind of desperate person needs an eighty-seven-year-old kidney?"

The absurdity of her suggestion made Paula blush. "I only said I'd heard something. I'm not saying it's right."

I grinned at her. "Hey, no idea is too far out there. I'm not picky at this point. Did Gus say anything else about Ron's situation?"

"Just that if something doesn't change, Druther's might have to close."

"Ron took the place over after his dad died, didn't he?"

Paula nodded. "I think he did it out of loyalty to his father. Gus said he's never really been happy running the business."

"Well, I still don't see how substituting one body for another helps his money woes. It doesn't make sense."

Just then the waitress brought our food. The aroma of quiche Lorraine drifted up into my nostrils. I prayed quietly over my food and then stuck my fork into the flaky, cheesy concoction. My taste buds confirmed what my nose already knew. It was yummy.

"Hilde," Paula said frowning, "you've talked a lot about the fact that Mabel has gone missing. But what about the other side of it?"

I shook my head. "What other side?"

"Well, you're missing one body. But what about the woman Druther's is trying to pass off as Mabel?"

Paula was right. I'd almost forgotten her. "I. . .I don't know. But someone should be looking for her. Have you heard any rumbles about anyone else who's wandered off?"

She laughed. "No, no misplaced bodies that I know of. I think that kind of information would get around."

I took another bite, chewed, and swallowed. "So what do I do, Paula? I can't ignore this. I have to find a way to clear my name before the meeting next Friday, and I have to figure out who that woman is that's being buried as Mabel."

Paula scooped up some granola and yogurt with her spoon and stared at it. Then she sighed and shook her head. "I don't know what to tell you. At this point you have no evidence whatsoever. You can't prove anything."

"I know," I agreed. "It's Ron's word against mine."

"And her family's," Paula said.

"They're the only ones who can fix this. They've got to take a look inside that coffin. Then someone has to find Mabel."

Paula swirled her long spoon around inside her glass. "This certainly isn't going to make Druther's look good."

"Paula, I've done everything I can to help them avoid a scandal. But Ron won't pay any attention to me. That's why I have to wonder if he's involved somehow."

"But surely he'd realize he can't keep this hidden."

I stared into my friend's dark green eyes. "Something bothers me about having the casket closed. Why? There's not any disfiguration that would usually explain a closed casket. What if this is Ron's way of keeping anyone from seeing the body before it's buried?"

"But Hilde," Paula said, waving her spoon at me, "that's not the decision of the funeral director. The family makes that decision."

"I know. But it certainly seems convenient, doesn't it?"

"Yes. Yes, it does. Maybe you should contact the family yourself and suggest that they take a gander at the dearly departed Mabel."

"What do I do? Call them up on the phone and say, 'Oh, by the way. Your beloved aunt has gone missing, and you're getting ready to bury a stranger. Would you mind taking a peek?' Not really something a family wants to hear on the day they plan to say good-bye to their loved one."

"Not any more than 'Oh, by the way, do you mind if we dig your aunt up just to make sure we buried the right person?'"

"I see your point."

"So now what?" Paula finished her yogurt and stared at my quiche.

I promptly stuck the last two bites in my mouth before she asked me for some. Paula likes to order something healthy then finish her lunch up with whatever I'm eating. I rarely get to complete my meals when we dine together. Usually it's okay. But this quiche was just too good to share. "I'm going to talk to Gwen tonight. After that, I'll decide what to do. If she won't help me, I'll call the family, I guess."

Paula grinned. "You could call them anonymously—from a pay phone. There's no reason to tell them who you are."

"Great idea." I couldn't keep the sarcasm out of my voice. "Since I'm the only one saying that Mabel isn't Mabel, no one will figure out who the call came from."

"Look at it this way. When the family discovers the truth, you'll be the hero of the day."

"Maybe. But right now I'd settle for Mabel finding her way home. Even if I have nothing to do with it."

Paula nodded. Then she grimaced. "I just thought of something. How can you be sure the first woman you saw *was* Mabel? Maybe the first body was tagged wrong, and the woman you worked on really is Mabel."

A shiver of trepidation ran down my spine. I hadn't thought of that. Then I remembered something. "It can't be. The woman in the picture had a natural part on the left side. The woman I worked on had a natural part in the middle. If the woman in the picture was Mabel, and her family said it was, the part's wrong."

Paula leaned back against the booth seat. "Wow. You're like the Sherlock of locks. They could make a weekly series around you."

I laughed. "I don't think anyone's looking for a detective hairstylist for the dead, but thanks for the vote of confidence."

I glanced at my watch and realized that Paula's lunch hour was drawing to a close. So far, all we'd done was talk about my problems. "Thanks for all the input," I said, "but tell me how you're doing. How are things going with your new boyfriend?"

As soon as the words left my mouth, I knew I shouldn't have said them. When Paula was *in love*, I always heard about it as soon as we sat down. Last time we'd met for lunch, she was seeing a man she'd met at one of her *enlightened* group meetings. According to her, they were madly in love. What was his name? Brent? Brian?

"I'm not seeing Brad anymore." The statement was said in a matter-of-fact manner, but I knew Paula well enough to know that once again her heart had been broken.

"What happened?" I asked gently.

Paula's eyes filled with tears—not something that happened very often. This breakup must have really hurt. "He—he said there was too much negativity in my soul. That we weren't in tune anymore."

"Oh." Well, here was a whole new way to break up with someone. I guess it sounded a little more spiritual than "It's not you; it's me." I could see on Paula's face that the effect was just as devastating. "I'm sorry, Paula. I really am. You know, you might try that singles group at church I was telling you about. . . ."

"I told you I'm not interested, Hilde," she said with a sigh. "Why do you keep bringing it up?"

I wanted to yell at her. I wanted to scream, "Because you need God!" But I didn't. I just smiled and shook my head.

With a tear snaking down her cheek, she reached over and took my hand. "I've told you before that I respect the divine in you. Why can't you accept the divine in me? I'm happy and content for the first time in my life."

She certainly didn't look happy and content. She looked

miserable. I pulled up my courage. "Look, Paula. I'm not telling you what to do, but I worry about you. There isn't any way to have the 'divine' inside you without God. You need Him. Not some new age substitute. He's the only One who can actually get inside and heal you. And He's the only One who can turn your life around."

She pulled her hand away and sat back in her seat. Her eyes narrowed. "Sorry. I've seen your God. He's too judgmental. I could never be what He wants me to be."

I smiled. "He knows that, Paula. That's why He doesn't ask you to change. He simply asks that you let Him inside so He can do the changing." I could tell from the way her body stiffened that I'd gone too far. "All right. I'll stop. But just remember what I told you. God loves you completely—without reservation. He's the father you've always wanted—and more. I should know. My father took off a long time ago with his girlfriend, and he's never cared enough in all these years to contact me or pay one penny of child support. But my heavenly Father was there all the time, loving me and taking care of me. And He's waiting for you to give Him a chance. Any time." I grinned at her. "And it just so happens that I love you, too, you goofy nut."

Her shoulders relaxed, and I knew we'd moved past the awkwardness—again. "I know you love me, Hilde. Thanks. I love you, too."

The waitress came over with our bill. I took it from her before Paula could reach for it. "It's on me today. I owe you for all the good advice."

She smiled. "Thanks. Next time it's my treat."

I slid my debit card into the check holder, and Paula and I gabbed about other things going on in our lives while we waited for the waitress to pick it up. I learned that Paula's parents were moving out of town. She seemed relieved. I could understand that. While she talked, I thought about the relationship between her and her parents—and me and my mother. Was it so very different? My mother and I were both Christians, but we weren't communicating any better than Paula and her mother and father. Not a very good witness. Seemed to me that even though my mom and I had different personalities, we should still be able to share our common faith.

When we got up to leave, I hugged Paula good-bye and promised to call her after my meeting with Gwen. I drove back to Eden, thankful the roads weren't too bad. Before I went home, however, I drove two blocks past the boardinghouse to the Garden of Eden Bookstore. Actually, it's really not much more than Ida Mae's front room, filled with used books. She'd hung a curtain up between the store and the rest of her house. Besides the large shelves that line the walls, there are always tables scattered around with signs that advertise SPECIALS! These are books that Ida Mae marks down because no one has bought them and she needs the space for newer used books. I'd found some great bargains on those tables. I suspect she stashes away a special pile of mysteries just for me. When I pull up in front of the bookstore, she takes a few of them out and tosses them on the tables for me to *discover*. Ida Mae is a generous soul who lives on Social Security, a small pension from the railroad where her husband worked, and the proceeds from the small amount of books she sells every month. But she doesn't run the bookstore just for the money. She loves books. Being able to share her favorites with other people makes her happy. She also loves the visitors her little store brings in. The Garden of Eden Bookstore gives her a purpose and brings her fulfillment. And what more could any of us ask of life?

I dropped off a large bag of books my mother had sent along for Ida Mae, and I picked up two new mysteries the elderly woman had put aside for me. She stood in her doorway, waving good-bye as I backed out of her driveway. I promised myself that I would go back soon and spend more time with her. Her customers dwindle when the weather gets bad, and she was probably lonely for some company. Right now, though, I needed a quick nap before my date tonight.

As I parked my car, I thought about how interesting this evening promised to be. A date with Adam and a chance to find out from Gwen what was really going on at Druther's. Hopefully I would be one step closer to finding Mabel and putting her back where she belonged.

CHANGE †† ††† SEVEN

"Two orders of Sweet and Spicy Three Ingredients. She'd like hers mild. And could you bring us an order of crab rangoon as an appetizer?"

A simple request in my favorite restaurant, and the whole showering naked together debacle was pushed into the dark recesses of my mind. Hopefully it would stay there. This man liked Sweet and Spicy Three Ingredients. That meant he was pretty close to perfect in my book.

The smiling waiter took our order and left. I glanced down at the tabletop in our booth. Colorful painted fish swam across it. They were mirrored by a beautiful mural on the wall next to us. Easy-listening music played in the background. My afternoon nap and the atmosphere in the restaurant combined to make me feel relaxed yet alert. Usually evenings were spent in my apartment, cuddled up under my grandmother's quilt in my comfortable chair—with my current mystery novel. I almost always fell asleep within thirty minutes of opening the first page.

Adam smiled at me, his azure eyes locked on mine. I didn't feel uncomfortable though. It wasn't like he was staring at me. It was more like he was *seeing* me. And for some reason, I felt that he liked what he saw. I hoped I wouldn't do something stupid that would drive that look away. It had happened before. I'd been on several first dates. A few second dates. But usually after that, the guy never called again. I'm not really certain why. My mother tells me it's because I'm not confident enough—that other people can't have faith in you if you don't have any in yourself. Maybe she's right. But I prayed that this time there would be more dates. A lot more.

"So tell me what it's like to be a stockbroker," I said. "You're the only one I've ever known."

He shrugged. "I'm afraid there's not much to tell. I advise clients on what stocks to buy. They buy them, and either they make money, or they lose money. That's about it."

"But you have to really understand the market, right?"

"Well, it certainly helps," he said with a grin, "but in the end, it's just a guessing game."

I'd hoped my questions would stir up some discussion, but it didn't look like we were going much further on that topic. I was at a disadvantage, since I knew nothing about the stock market.

"So do you enjoy what you do?" I asked, scrambling for something else to say.

Adam paused while the waiter brought our coffee to the

table. When he left, Adam added cream to his cup and stirred it, not saying anything. Great. I'd brought that conversation to a screeching halt.

Finally he looked up at me. "You know, Hilde. One of the things I like about you so much is that you have the ability to get to the heart of a situation. You did that when we were kids. Like the time you said that the only reason I kept striking out in baseball was because I didn't believe I could hit the ball. You told me to say, 'I can hit the baseball,' over and over until I believed it. I did what you suggested, and before long I started hitting the ball." He reached over and took my hand. "I went to college on a baseball scholarship. I credit you with that. I always have."

I was flabbergasted. To be honest, I didn't even remember giving Adam that advice. To find out that I had impacted someone's life without knowing it startled me. "I—I don't know what to say, Adam. I had no idea." I could feel my ears burning. I wasn't used to this much praise. It was humbling, to say the least. Then I thought of something. "But you're a stockbroker, not a ballplayer. What happened?"

He squeezed my hand and then let it go. "A bad slide into home broke my leg and changed my plans. So I entered the business world. Not much of a connection there, but it's a living."

"Forgive me for saying this, but you don't seem very happy about your chosen profession. So why do you do it?"

He smiled. "You asked if I enjoy my job. I don't hate it.

It's got its good points and its bad points. I don't get the kind of satisfaction from buying stocks that I got from baseball, but it pays the bills and provides me with enough money to do the thing I really love."

"And that is?"

He shook his head. "Nope. I'm not going to tell you. I have to show you. This Saturday I'll pick you up around nine in the morning. You'll get to see what's really important to me."

A second date? And we hadn't even finished the first one yet. Wow. I was ahead of the game. "Okay. Sounds good."

"Now," Adam said with a grin, "let's make this evening more interesting. Tell me about *your* job. I want to know how you got started and why you do it. I'm quite certain we'll both find it more stimulating than the stock market."

I began by telling him about Monsieur Maximilian and Maximilian's Salon de L'Elégance. He seemed to get a real kick out of it. A few times, I even made myself laugh. Strange how something that seems kind of awful at the time can get funny the further you get away from it. Too bad we can't always see the humor when it's happening. By the time I got to Mrs. Maitland's funeral, the waiter brought our food. Adam offered to pray over it before I said a word. Another point for our side. After taking a few bites of one of the best meals in town, I went back to my story. Even though I hadn't intended to disclose my current situation, it came tumbling out. Perhaps it was because I'd already told Gabe. It was easier this time, especially since Gabe's reaction hadn't been to look at me with suspicion. As soon as I started talking about Mabel and the diamond ring, though, I realized I might have made a mistake. I didn't want to date Gabe. I brought the story to a quick conclusion, watching Adam's expression.

He put his fork down and gaped at me. Was he regretting his invitation to dinner? Was our date already over before it even started?

"Oh, Hilde," he said, his face tight. "That's awful. Someone's obviously trying to frame you. The only question is why."

Relief washed over me. "That's just what Gabe said. So you believe me?"

Adam frowned. "Of course I believe you. Who's Gabe?"

I leaned back in my seat. "You know, I'm beginning to feel a lot better about this whole thing. At first I felt so guilty— even though I knew I hadn't taken the ring. Then I started to worry that no one would believe me. But so far, the only person who thinks I'm a thief seems to be Ron Druther."

"People who know you will believe you, Hilde. Now who's Gabe?"

"I guess you're right. Even my mother believed me, even though she still had to get in a jab about my job. Maybe this situation won't be as bad as—"

"Would you please, please tell me who this Gabe person is?" Adam interrupted, his tone sharp.

I stopped and stared at him. "What?"

He took a deep breath and blew air out slowly between

clenched teeth. "For the last time, who is Gabe?"

I realized that Adam Sawyer—good-looking Adam Sawyer, the successful stockbroker, the man who liked Sweet and Spicy Three Ingredients and prayed before he ate—*was jealous*! Of Gabe Bashevis! I couldn't help it. I started to giggle.

"Hilde Higgins," Adam hissed. "I don't know what you find so funny. If you're involved with someone else, I would simply like to know."

"No. The answer is no. Gabriel Bashevis must be close to seventy years old. He lives across the street from my boardinghouse. Although he is a rather nice-looking man, I don't have any romantic feelings toward him."

Adam's face flushed. "Well, of course you may see whomever you wish. It's not my business. I simply wondered who this man is. I don't. . . ."

"I wish you'd stop right there." I stared down at my plate, afraid to watch his expression. "I like that you care about whether or not I'm seeing someone else."

Silence. Had I said too much? In some ways it felt as if we were moving really fast. Yet in another way, I felt more comfortable with Adam than I'd ever felt with any man. It was almost like we'd simply picked up where we left off years ago. Best friends then. Best friends now.

"Hilde," Adam said, his voice almost a whisper. "I—I. . ."

I felt my face get hot. "I'm sorry. I've said something inappropriate and made you uncomfortable."

"Hilde, look at me. . .please."

I brought my head up and found myself gazing into his eyes. What I saw there wasn't embarrassment.

He looked away for a moment and shook his head. Then he looked at me again. "Look, it's not my intention to make things awkward, but I really feel the need to be honest."

My heart skipped a beat. Uh-oh. This was it. The "let's just be friends" speech. I'd heard it before. Of course, you were never friends after that.

"The last time I saw you, we were thirteen years old. The day you moved away was the worst day of my life. And every day since then I've wondered about you." He sighed, and his incredible blue eyes seemed to peer straight into my soul. "Every girl I've known since then has been compared to you. And every single one of them has come up lacking. You see, even though I was only thirteen when you left, I was madly in love with you."

"We're not teenagers anymore, Adam. I'm not sure I'm the same person I used to be. People change." His words filled me with fear. What Adam had felt for me wasn't love; it was nothing more than a schoolboy crush. To be honest, I'd had a pretty big crush on him, too, even though I'd never told him. The problem was that the girl I saw when I looked back in time wasn't the same woman who sat across from him now. When my father walked out, insecurity pushed that girl away. Adam was looking for someone who barely existed anymore.

"I know that," he said. "I want to get to know who you

are now. And you need to get to know me. I've changed, too."
He reached past my plate and grabbed my hand again. "I'm
willing to give us a chance to get reacquainted. Are you?"

"I'd like that. I only hope you like the woman I've
become."

Adam smiled, breaking the serious tone we'd set. "So far
I'm not the least bit disappointed. How about you?"

I shook my head. "No. I'm not disappointed either."

He grinned and let go of my hand. "Good. Now let's
finish this great meal and see what we can do about your
problem."

"I don't intend to drag you into this mess," I said, spearing
a big piece of delectable shrimp.

"I'm already dragged. You said the funeral directors are all
meeting next Friday?"

I nodded while I chewed.

"We don't have much time. What's your next step?"

I washed the shrimp down with coffee. "I'm glad you
brought that up." I checked my watch. "I'm meeting with
Gwen Cox from Druther's in about forty minutes. I'm sorry
to cut our evening short, but she's leaving town tomorrow,
and this was the only time she could talk to me. I'm hoping
she can tell me something that will help."

"I understand." Adam drummed his fingers on the table
and frowned. "Where are you meeting her?"

"At the Starbucks near Druther's."

"I have an idea. Why don't I drive you over there? I work

at Harris, Pringle & Sanders. It's right down the street from Starbucks. I left some papers there that I need over the weekend. I was going to drive over tomorrow and pick them up, but this will save me a trip. This way we can discuss what you find out, and our night won't have to end so early. I'll drive you back here later to pick up your car."

I agreed, happy that I would get to spend more time with him. I was also glad to have someone to talk to after speaking to Gwen. Hopefully she would tell me something that would put me closer to finding the truth.

Adam quickly finished his dinner. As usual, I couldn't eat an entire order. The waiter put the leftovers in a box and brought us our check, along with two fortune cookies. Adam started to reach for a cookie, but I stopped him.

"You're supposed to take the cookie closest to you," I scolded him with a smile. "That's the fortune meant for you."

He laughed and handed me the cookie he'd picked up. "Sorry. I guess I don't know the proper etiquette for fortune cookies. I won't make that mistake again." He pulled out his billfold and put a credit card on the bill tray. Then he took the cookie nearest him. "You read yours first."

I took off the wrapper and broke the cookie in half, pulling out the fortune. When I gazed down at it, I could hardly believe my eyes. I quickly stuck the small piece of paper under my saucer. "It's too silly to read," I said, hoping he'd take my word for it. "You read yours."

He frowned. "Goodness, Hilde. What did it say?"

I was afraid my face was the color of a ripe tomato. "Please, Adam. Just read yours."

Before I knew it, he reached over and pulled the fortune out from underneath the saucer, where I'd obviously done a rotten job of hiding it. "Got it! Now what's so bad about this. . . ." As he looked at it, he started to smile. " 'The love you've been waiting for is closer than you think.' " Adam folded the piece of paper up and put it in his pocket. "If you don't mind, I think I'll keep this. I've always thought fortune cookies were silly. Until today."

I was so embarrassed I just shook my head. The situation felt like a setup. If I didn't know better, I'd suspect that my mother was in the kitchen, writing out fortunes and paying the restaurant staff to deliver her handiwork. The waiter came over and picked up the bill tray. He seemed amused. I wondered if he'd overheard us.

"Don't get self-conscious on me," Adam said with a chuckle after the waiter walked away. "It's just a fortune cookie. It doesn't really mean anything. I'm sorry I teased you. You can have it back if you want."

"No. You can keep it." I grabbed my water glass. There might be snow outside, but I felt incredibly warm. I took a couple of gulps and set it down. "You haven't read yours." I tried to sound nonchalant, but my voice was a little higher than normal.

Adam snapped his cookie open and read the fortune. He broke into a wide grin. " 'Prepare for an unexpected change.

Your future holds many surprises.'" He held the fortune out to me. "Here. I took yours. You can have mine. No stockbroker is looking for unexpected changes. Maybe our cookies got mixed up after all. Your fortune cookie–placement rule seems to have let you down."

I took the slip of paper from his hand and put it in my purse. "I really think I've had enough unexpected surprises for a while."

Adam laughed. "That's for sure. Let's get you over to Starbucks. I hope you find out something that will help us."

I slid out of the booth. Adam took my coat and held it out for me. I noticed that he'd used the word *us*. It made me feel good to know I wasn't alone, but it still seemed odd to have someone step into my life so quickly. I wasn't certain how I felt about it. I was bouncing back and forth between exultation and caution. I didn't seem to know which emotion to lock on to.

When we got outside, Adam pointed to a silver Lexus parked near the front door. Being a stockbroker obviously paid well. He held the door open for me. His manners had improved since the days of trying to get me to eat bugs and dirt. We talked about our parents on the ride over to Starbucks. I was glad to hear that both his parents were healthy and living happily in a retirement community in Florida.

We talked a little about my mother. I told him that she was very successful, but I didn't mention that we didn't get along very well. There'd been enough revelations for one night. I'd just started to tell him about my apartment in Eden when I heard sirens behind us. Adam pulled over and waited for two big fire engines and an emergency vehicle to pass us. They didn't go far, just a couple of blocks ahead.

"What is it?" I asked, straining my neck to see around traffic. "Can you see what's on fire?"

"Not yet. And it looks like we're not going to get very close."

Two police cars blocked the intersection in front of us. Officers were directing traffic away from the block the fire was on.

"Adam, turn left and go around to the next intersection. Then we can go west a couple of blocks and come back up the street. I don't want to keep Gwen waiting."

He pulled the car into the left-turn lane. As we rounded the corner, I could finally see exactly where the fire was. Druther's Funeral Home was fully engulfed in flames.

"Oh, Adam," was all I could say.

"I'm sure Gwen got out. We'll probably find her waiting for you at Starbucks. Let's not worry yet."

All I could do was pray while Adam maneuvered around the block and headed back toward the coffee shop. We pulled into the parking lot where quite a few people stood looking down the street toward the scene of the fire.

"Hilde, I'm going to wait here. You go in and see if Gwen is inside." Adam gave me a reassuring smile. I didn't feel quite so positive. I jumped out of the car and ran toward the building, glancing through the gathered crowd. Gwen wasn't among them. I pushed the glass door open with so much force I almost hit a man carrying a large coffee.

"Hey, watch it, little lady," he said gruffly. "I'm not lookin' to get baptized today." Luckily he had a lid on his cup so the liquid didn't splash onto his leather jacket. It looked like a custom job. Ruining it could have cost me a week's salary. I apologized quickly and rushed past him, carefully scanning the store. No Gwen. I hurried up to the counter and asked the clerk if she had seen anyone who looked like Gwen. I described her and waited.

"Sounds like you're talking about Gwen Cox," the woman said. "She comes in here all the time, but she hasn't been in this evening. I'd remember." She shook her head. "I wouldn't worry about her, miss. She hardly ever works this late. I'm sure she went home a long time ago."

I thanked her and left the building. By the time I got back to Adam's car, I couldn't hold back my tears. I opened the door and got in. "She's not there, Adam. What if. . .what if she. . ." I couldn't finish my sentence.

"You stay here," he said with a frown. "Let me see if I can get closer and find out something."

He got out of the car and began walking down the sidewalk. While he was gone, I prayed for Gwen. Although faith should never be defined by feelings, there have been times in my life when something inside me told me my prayer was too late. I tried hard to ignore that impression now.

After what felt like a long time, Adam got back to the car. "I told a guy from the fire department that someone might still be inside," he said as he climbed back into his seat. "They don't know anything yet. Until they get things under control some, they can't look for anyone." He slapped the steering wheel out of frustration. "That old building should have been pulled down years ago. Frankly, it was an accident waiting to happen." He reached over and put his hand on my shoulder. "Listen, no one would tell me anything, but I overheard one fireman tell a police officer that the fire looked suspicious."

"Suspicious?" I echoed. "You mean they think it might be arson?"

"It's too early to tell. There'll be an investigation, but they seem to think there's some reason to suspect it." Adam turned up the heater. It had grown colder outside, and snow was beginning to drift lazily from the sky. The flashing lights from emergency vehicles filled the car, causing the interior to glow and pulsate. I tried not to think about how the pattern reminded me of a beating heart.

"Listen, Hilde," Adam said with a frown, "if this *is* arson, it puts a whole different complexion on this situation. I think it's time to talk to the police."

I shook my head. "What situation? An accusation of a stolen ring that isn't stolen? A body that no one but me thinks is missing? What does that have to do with the fire? I don't have anything to tell the police that makes sense."

"What if Gwen *was* in the building? Then what?"

"I hope with everything inside me that she wasn't, but I have no way to connect her to Mabel or the ring. If Gwen's gone, then I'll never know if she had something important to tell me. And I certainly can't come up with any reason for someone to burn down Druther's."

"But don't you find it a strange coincidence?"

I sighed and looked down the street where flames still licked the sky. "Of course I do, but there's no way to prove anything now. No way to confirm that the woman being called Mabel is actually someone else. That body is probably a pile of ashes."

Even as I said it, a chill wriggled through my body. *Was* the fire an unfortunate accident? Or had events just taken a dark and deadly turn?

CHAPTER ⚏ EIGHT

Adam and I waited around for over an hour after the fire was brought under control, but we couldn't get any information about Gwen. One fire investigator did ask me about our meeting. I told him everything except why we were supposed to get together. I didn't get home until a little after midnight. Then I fell into bed and was bombarded with troubled dreams about fire and dead bodies walking around calling my name. I woke up a little after seven when my phone rang. I rolled over and picked it up from the nightstand next to the bed. A glance at my caller ID told me it was Adam. I hesitated a moment before answering. I was pretty sure he was going to tell me something I didn't want to hear. Finally I gave in.

"Hilde," he said in a solemn voice after I said hello, "it's not good news."

I couldn't control the catch in my voice. "I know. I think I knew it all along."

"Look, I don't have to go into the office today. Why don't

you let me come by and pick you up? We can have breakfast somewhere and talk."

I appreciated the offer, but right then I didn't want to see anyone. Especially Adam. I could feel a pretty good cry coming on, and I wasn't comfortable enough yet to do that in front of him. "Thanks, but I think I'd like to be alone for a while." I realized that he hadn't actually told me anything specific. "What exactly did you hear, and who said it?"

"It was on the early morning news. One death is reported, but they haven't named her yet. Not until they contact the next of kin. I called a client who works for the police department. He told me privately that they already know it's Gwen Cox. You can't repeat that, Hilde. Not until her name is released to the public."

I could feel tears begin to run down the sides of my face while I stared up at the ceiling. "Anything else?" I croaked out, trying not to fall apart with Adam listening. "Did the entire structure burn down?"

Adam was silent for a moment. "Do you really want the details?"

I nodded before I realized he couldn't see me. "Might as well tell me. I'll find out eventually."

He cleared his throat. "It was pretty much a total loss. The main fire started in the back where they keep the chemicals."

"But—but Gwen wouldn't have been back there. Where did they find her?"

"My contact said she was discovered near the spot where they think the fire started. I don't know what room she was in; he didn't say. But he did mention that all the bodies were a complete loss except for one in a viewing room near the front of the building."

My mind felt like a computer trying to put all the information together into something that made sense. Why would Gwen be in the back room? She had nothing to do with preparing the bodies. "She should have been in her office. She told me she had paperwork to do before her vacation."

"Maybe she was trying to put out the fire," Adam offered.

"I guess anything's possible. . . ."

"Could the body in the viewing room be the same one Druther's said was Mabel?"

"No. Mabel's service was a closed casket. She wouldn't be in a viewing room. That had to be Mr. Gonzalez or Mr. Nguyen. They're the only two clients who'd been there long enough to be ready for a viewing."

Although Adam's information had momentarily distracted me, I could feel the need to bawl getting stronger. "Listen Adam, thanks for the information. And thanks for sticking it out with me last night. I need to get off the phone now."

"Hilde, call me if you need anything. If you want to talk, I'm here."

The concern in his voice only made me feel more emotional. "Th–thanks. I—I really need to go now."

"Okay. If I don't hear from you sooner, I'll see you tomorrow at nine. Dress comfortably but nice. Bye."

I tried to stop him before he hung up, but all I heard was the dial tone in my ear. I doubted I would feel like going anywhere in the morning. I got out of bed, grabbed a box of tissues, and let my bruised emotions pour out. I sobbed so hard I got the hiccups. I'd moved on to holding my breath in an attempt to control them when my phone rang again. I started to ignore it but at the last second decided to see who was calling. WILLOWBROOK, the caller ID read. Paula. I clicked YES.

"Paula?" I said right before my next hiccup.

"Hilde, is that you?" she said, her voice almost a whisper.

"Yes. I've got the—*yurp*—hiccups."

"Listen, I've got to make this quick. I want you to come down and work on someone this morning."

"Oh, Paula. I don't think I can—*yurp*—do that this morning. Didn't you hear about the fire at Druther's?"

"Yes," she hissed. "That's why I'm calling you. Mabel Winnemaker's family has moved the funeral here. It's at eleven this morning. They said they didn't want to delay it any longer, because of some out-of-town relatives. The remains have been sent to us, and the service is going to be in our chapel. If you come down, you might be able to talk to someone about Mabel. You can't tell Gus, though. He's a great guy, but he wouldn't want you bothering the family with weird questions."

"Paula, do you really have a—*yurp*—client for me?"

She laughed softly. "Not really, but if we get caught, I'll just say it was a mistake."

I considered her offer. It would most likely be my last chance to stop Mabel's family from burying someone else in her grave. "Okay, I'll come. Uh, Paula. Just how much did they—I mean, what kind of—*yurp*. . ."

"How much of the phony Mabel's remains remain?"

Trust Paula to put it like that. "Yes. That's what I mean."

"Not much, Hilde. Any more damage, and there wouldn't have been anything left to bury. That old wooden building was a firetrap if I've ever seen one. Gus and some of the other directors have been after Ron for years to tear it down and build something safer." She paused for a moment. "You know, Hilde, with Ron's financial problems, this was odd timing. Gus didn't say it, but I know he's wondering if this fire was Ron's attempt to solve his money woes."

"I—I can't believe he'd do something like that. I mean, no matter how hard he is to get along with, I still think he cares about the funeral home and its tradition."

"You'd be surprised what someone might be willing to do when their back is against the wall."

"Maybe so. I guess I don't know people very well. So what time do I need to be there?"

"Around ten thirty. And come in the side door. I'll wait for you. No sense announcing to Gus that you're here."

"But how are you going to get me around Mabel's family

without Gus knowing?"

"You let me worry about that. All you have to do is show up."

Paula's tone was familiar to me. It meant: *Don't argue. Just do what I tell you to do.* Sometimes her take-charge attitude is good. Sometimes, not so much. But today I decided to go with it. Meeting Mabel's relatives at the service meant I wouldn't have to go to their home. Something I'd rather not do.

I told Paula I'd be there and hung up. Then I lay in bed awhile longer, trying to decide if I was all cried out. I still felt an overwhelming sadness about Gwen, but questions were filling my thoughts, pushing out my grief. Was the fire arson? If it was, who set it and why? Was it to hide the truth about Mabel, or was it Ron Druther's way to get out of his money problems? Whatever the answer, hoping the family would notice that Mabel wasn't Mabel was impossible now.

I finally got out of bed, fed Sherlock, and took a shower. I stood under the hot water a little longer than usual. It felt great and loosened me up a little. After I got out, I took my time brushing my teeth and putting on my makeup. I had just gotten dressed when I heard someone talking in the bathroom. It was more than a little startling, but it only took a couple of seconds for me to realize that the voice was drifting up through the vent in the floor. It had to be coming from one of the rooms below me. Mrs. Hudson had recently had some work done on the old heating system in the house. It was definitely warmer now, but it appeared that

somehow the pipes were sending out more than just heat. I
didn't have any plan to listen until another voice joined the
first, agitated and angry. Although eavesdropping isn't a very
attractive activity, I told myself it was concern for whoever
was involved that led me to get down on my hands and knees
and stick my ear against the floor register. At first I couldn't
tell who the voices belonged to. Gradually I realized it was
Mrs. Hudson and Minnie. I could only make out certain
words and phrases, but Mrs. Hudson was certainly upset
about something. Were the two friends having a fight?

I heard Mrs. Hudson say "just a thief" and "call the
police." Then Minnie said "catch him in the act." There was
some other mumbled conversation, and then Mrs. Hudson
said something about "where he goes every day." They had to
be talking about Isaiah Sims. He was the only person who left
the house daily. Did Mrs. Hudson think he was stealing?

I stood up and gathered my things to take back to my
room. I wished I hadn't been so nosy. I liked Isaiah, and I
certainly didn't think he'd be involved in anything criminal.
At least for now, I decided to put my concerns about the
conversation I'd overheard on the back burner. I had way
too many things on the front burners. If I wasn't careful, the
stove in my mind was going to catch fire.

I made my favorite breakfast: grilled SPAM® with Bacon,
scrambled eggs, and cheddar cheese on a bagel. By the time
I finished breakfast and downed two cups of coffee, I felt
a little better. A glance out the window at the dark clouds

blanketing the city told me that more snow was on the way. I wondered if it would hamper the investigators who were trying to determine the cause of the fire. Even though it looked suspicious, I hoped it wasn't. There wasn't any reason for arson that wouldn't be awful. Whether someone was trying to hide the truth about Mabel or whether Ron Druther burned down his own funeral home for money, it was a terrible outcome for everyone—especially Gwen and her family.

I looked across the street at Gabe's place then glanced at my watch. I had plenty of time before I had to meet Paula. I decided to run over and see him.

I pulled on my coat, waved good-bye to Sherlock, and went downstairs. I could hear Mrs. Hudson and Minnie in the kitchen, but I went straight to the front door, not wanting to interrupt them. I'd just put my hand on the doorknob when I heard someone clear his throat. Isaiah had come down the stairs behind me. His thin frame was covered with an old, black wool coat that had seen better days, but he was bundled up with what looked like several layers of clothing. He was certainly well protected against the cold. A knit cap covered his head, and he was pulling on a pair of aged leather gloves while he clutched a paper lunch sack under his arm.

"Looks like more snow," he said to me with a slight smile.

"Yes, it does. You should be warm though."

He shuffled slowly over to the door. "These old bones feel the cold a lot more than they used to. I try to wrap up as much as I can." He looked me over and shook his head. "You should get a heavier coat, young lady."

I held the door open for him while he finished putting on his last glove. "Just don't tell my mother I'm not wearing the new coat she bought me. It's warmer than this one, but I wouldn't be caught dead in it."

He chuckled. "You young people pick looks over wisdom sometimes." He grinned at me. "But I'm not so old I don't remember my mother yelling at me to button my coat and cover my head. I hated it, too."

I laughed as he stepped out onto the porch. I turned around to close the door behind us and saw Mrs. Hudson staring at me from the kitchen entrance. Her mouth was tight, and her arms were crossed against her ample chest. When she noticed me looking at her, she gave me a quick smile and stepped back into the kitchen. I suspected her hostility was directed toward Isaiah. I hoped she wouldn't ask him to leave. Isaiah reminded me of a man who used to show up every day at a diner near school when I was in college. He'd order a cup of coffee, but he never bought anything to eat. He just sat at the counter for a couple of hours, talking to the staff. I asked the waitress about him once. She'd smiled and said, "He just needs a place to belong, honey. We all do." That was Isaiah Sims. A man who needed a place to belong.

I said good-bye to Isaiah and watched him get into his old compact car. It took several attempts to get it going, but finally he pulled slowly out of the small parking area on the side of the house. Mrs. Hudson keeps her car in the garage, and the rest of us park on a cement lot created just for residents. There's a metal cover mounted on poles that keeps the snow and rain off our cars—unless it's windy. Not a perfect solution, but I'm grateful for it.

I drove across the street to Gabe's, curious to find out his take on what had happened. I parked the car and trudged up to the door. The eternal OPEN sign was in the window, so I turned the doorknob. It was unlocked. As usual, the shop was dark. I started to call Gabe's name, but surprisingly I found him seated behind the counter, staring at me.

"Goodness," I said with a smile, "you startled me. If you sit there very often, people might start to think you're actually serious about running a business."

He had on a pair of thick, black-framed reading glasses. They sat on the end of his nose, and he peered over the top of them at me. "And what makes you think I'm not serious?"

"Well, let me see," I said while closing the door behind me. "Your sign outside is faded and almost ready to fall off. You never clear the snow off your parking lot. There aren't ever any lights on in here. You—"

"Never mind. Forget I asked." He took his glasses off. "And what can I do for you? Or did you just come over here to tell me what a rotten businessman I am?"

"No. I actually had something else in mind. I'd ask if you were busy, but that would really be a waste of time, wouldn't it?"

He folded his arms and frowned at me. "You're getting pretty cocky, aren't you?"

I took off my jacket and placed it over one of the bear's arms. "No, not really. Guess I just figure we're friends now." I said it lightheartedly, even though I didn't feel as confident as I sounded. Gabe Bashevis was an enigma. He acted as if he liked me, but I wasn't confident enough yet to take it for granted.

He stood up and shook his head. "Just what I need, a skinny little girl with a purple streak in her hair who sees dead people. It certainly proves that God has a sense of humor." He smiled at me. "Why don't we go upstairs and have a *cuppa,* as the English say."

I'd just had two cups of coffee, but Gabe's tea was so good that I happily agreed to his offer.

He slowly climbed the stairs, and I followed him. Again I was struck by the difference in his living quarters and the store downstairs. There was definitely a story here, although I could tell it was one I wouldn't find out about anytime soon. Gabe had his secrets, and we didn't know each other well enough yet for him to share them with me. I sat down at the kitchen table while he brewed the tea.

"So what's going on with your Mabel situation?" he asked casually. Obviously he hadn't heard about the fire. I was certain it was on the news. It dawned on me then that I hadn't seen a TV anywhere in his apartment. Was it possible he didn't have one?

I started at the beginning, which was lunch with Paula.

Then I moved on to dinner with Adam. Gabe asked about him, so I shared some general information. His name, what he did for a living, where he worked, and that he liked Sweet and Spicy Three Ingredients. I left out our past showering experience, our previous meals of slimy insects, and my feelings for him. I didn't think those facts were relevant. Then I poured out the rest of the story. Gabe didn't say anything, but his expression grew somber. He put a cup of tea in front of me and poured himself one. Then he sat down across from me.

"Hilde," he said finally, "you've got to take this turn of events very seriously." He fastened his dark eyes on mine. "You think the fire was started to cover the situation with Mabel or to collect insurance money?"

I shrugged. "I honestly don't know, but if it *is* arson, it's probably for one of those reasons." I took a sip of tea. "Wow. That's good. What is it?"

"It's English breakfast tea." He set his cup down. "Think this out with me. In either one of those scenarios, it wouldn't be necessary to kill this Gwen woman. If the funeral home owner wanted the insurance money, why would he risk everything by starting a fire with someone inside?"

I shrugged. "Maybe he didn't know?"

"Most arson fires are started in the early morning hours when no one is around. Not in the evening when the arsonist could be spotted. It doesn't make sense."

I took another sip of tea and contemplated this. "That

would have to apply to getting rid of the phony Mabel, too. Why not wait to start the fire? It wasn't like Mabel number two was going anywhere."

He nodded at me with a slight smile. "You've got it. Now tell me why someone would start a fire at such an inconvenient time. What was it they were actually targeting?"

I almost coughed up my tea. "Oh my goodness. Was Gwen the target?"

Gabe shook his head. "We really can't jump to that conclusion yet, but we should definitely add it to the mix."

"But why kill Gwen? Was there something important she wanted to tell me? Could someone have killed her to keep her from talking to me?" I slapped my hand on the table. "With Gwen gone, we might have lost our only chance to find out the truth."

"Not necessarily. Every criminal misses something. If you can find it, no matter how small the detail, you can solve your case. A wrong word, a forgotten fingerprint, something that doesn't belong—the littlest mistake can unlock the truth."

Gabe stared past me, lost in his thoughts. Suddenly his eyes widened, and he looked at me, a strange expression on his face. Mentally, I was stuck back at his comment about solving a case. What in the world was he talking about?

"S–Sorry. I read a lot of detective novels," he said. His face was flushed, and I began to worry that he was having another episode. I looked around the table but didn't see his pill bottle.

"That's okay," I said in an attempt to stave off another fainting spell. "I read a lot, too. Sometimes I find myself trying to think like Sherlock Holmes, Miss Marple, or Hercule Poirot."

This seemed to satisfy him, and his color began to return to normal. However, I still found his comments odd. "You'll never guess where I'm going," I said, purposely changing the subject. His raised eyebrow gave me the incentive I needed, and I told him about going to the other Mabel's service.

Gabe set his cup down so hard it rattled. "You be careful, Hilde." He stared at me, his eyebrows knitted together in a tight frown. "Why don't you simply tell these people your suspicions about Mabel and walk away? From here on out, it's up to them. You're out of it."

"How can I possibly be out of it? My reputation is still tarnished, and now Gwen's dead. I can't walk away."

"First of all, I don't think Ron Druther's first consideration is you anymore. He's lost his business, and he will probably find himself under suspicion of arson. Even if he goes to that meeting you're concerned about—and he might not—I don't think he'll be talking about you. And as far as Gwen Cox—you leave that to the fire investigators and the police. That's their job. If there was foul play, they'll find it."

For the first time in a while, I felt a twinge of hope. Maybe this nightmare was coming to an end. The police were better equipped for finding out what had happened than I was. Now that they were involved, perhaps it was best to stay out of it. "Okay. You're right. My last act on Mabel's behalf is to share my suspicions with her family. Then I'll leave it alone. Maybe life can get back to normal."

"Maybe," Gabe said rather absentmindedly.

I looked at my watch. "I need to get going. How about dinner tonight? I'll fix something and bring it over about six?" I had no intention of telling him that he would be the recipient of one of my famous SPAM® dishes. I found it was always better to let people taste it before telling them what it was. So far I'd never had anyone complain.

"Well," he said slowly, "I had thought about entertaining the queen this evening, but I suppose you'll just have to do."

I finished the tea in my cup and stood up. "I'm honored. I've never been preferred over the queen before. I'll bring my best manners."

"I should hope so," he said with a pronounced British accent. "Do you mind seeing yourself out? Think I'll stay up here and finish my tea."

I smiled at him. "I think I can find my way out. It's not all that complicated."

"I'm glad. I would have worried about you if you'd found it difficult."

I waved good-bye and was halfway through the living room when I heard him call my name. I turned around to see what he wanted.

"I just wanted to say. . . ." He cleared his throat and hesitated.

"Gabe?"

He turned in his chair toward me. "I just wanted to say that you're welcome here anytime. Just come on in like you own the place."

"Okay. Thanks." I started to say something humorous but realized that this was actually a rather serious moment. Gabe Bashevis was making a gesture of friendship, and it was important that I receive it in the manner he'd extended it. I smiled at him and left. I'd just reached the bottom of the stairs when I saw some papers lying on the floor next to the counter where he'd been sitting when I came in. The envelope I'd delivered to him was hanging off a shelf. It was obvious that it had been quickly shoved onto the shelf but hadn't been pushed in far enough. The contents had spilled out. For a moment I considered leaving everything where it was, but I easily convinced myself it would help Gabe if I cleaned up the mess. That still, small voice inside me tried to get my attention, but I ignored it. I glanced up the stairs to make sure Gabe was still in his apartment. Then I knelt down and retrieved several handwritten pages and an 8 x 10 photograph. The pages seemed to be a letter, but it wasn't written in English. I certainly wasn't a language expert, but thanks to Monsieur Max, I recognized that it was French. I sorted the pages into a neat stack and slid them back into the envelope but not before looking at the salutation and the signature. The letter was addressed to Gabriel. The signature belonged to a Catherine.

I picked up the picture, intending to slide it into the packet with the papers, but a couple of things caught my eye. The first thing I noticed was the two people in the photograph. One was obviously Gabe Bashevis, but he looked to be in his thirties or forties. I was right about his being handsome when he was younger. He reminded me of pictures I'd seen of Sean Connery at that age. And the woman beside him was breathtaking. She wore a long white dress with an oversize white hat. Beneath the circular rim was a cherubic face with dark eyes, a small turned-up nose, and the kind of lips women today only get through collagen injections. She was so beautiful I found myself staring at her, even though I was in a hurry. The smile on her face belonged to a woman who was truly loved and very happy. Her features were very familiar. I recognized her as the sad-looking woman in the painting that hung in Gabe's dining room. Gabe gazed down at her with a look of incredible tenderness. But as compelling as the picture was, what was written in red ink across the bottom of the photo was even more gripping. I may not know a lot of French, but I know what the word *meurtre* means. *Murder.*

I quickly slid the picture into the packet and placed it back on the shelf. Then I left as quickly and quietly as I could. All the way into Wichita, I wondered again just who Gabriel Bashevis, aka Gabriel Bastian, really was. Was his home the place of shelter and safety I'd imagined? Or had I actually put myself in a situation even more dangerous than the one I thought he was helping me to escape?

CHAPTER NINE

Iarrived at Willowbrook around ten o'clock, an hour before Mabel's service was to begin. I parked around the side of the building as Paula had requested. When I got out of the car, I saw her standing at the door, watching for me. I slipped in as quickly as I could and then followed her down the hall to her office.

"We're in the clear," she said once we'd reached our destination. "Gus isn't here. He's helping with a large service over at United Heights Church. Since the family said there would only be a few people attending Mabel's funeral and the nephew's giving the eulogy, Gus left me in charge here."

"Great. So I don't have to pretend I'm here to work?"

Paula shook her head. "Nope. You can sit in my office and drink coffee until after the service." She closed the door and grabbed a file folder from her desk. "It's sad. Most of Mabel's friends are gone. Besides the nephew and his wife, they don't expect more than a handful of people to attend. There's the grandson, but he won't be in town until Monday."

"I thought they had to have the funeral today because of out-of-town relatives."

"That was the intention, but the relatives from Nebraska got snowed in and couldn't come after all. The family decided to go ahead with the service so they could bury what's left of the poor woman."

"Well, that would make sense if Mabel Winnemaker was actually in that coffin!"

"Shush, Hilde! Man, when you get upset, your voice hits a pitch only dogs can hear."

"Sorry." My stomach felt tight. On the way to Willowbrook, I'd been relieved, since I planned to hand this whole mess over to Mabel's family. However, the reality of telling them that their late loved one had turned up "missing in action" seemed to be losing its appeal. How would they take it? First their aunt dies. Then she's toasted. Now some strange girl with a purple streak in her hair tells them their dear, dead aunt has actually disappeared and no one knows just where she is. Walking away and minding my own business began to look like a pretty good alternative. But I couldn't do it. Mabel deserved better than that.

"I've got to get ready for the service," Paula said. "You stay here until after it gets going then stand in the foyer. You can catch Alfred and Edith as they're leaving. But Hilde," Paula pointed one of her brightly colored fingernails at me. "You have to make it look like I'm not involved. Wait until I go back in the chapel before you approach them."

"Now wait a minute," I said, feeling like the wounded soldier left behind while his comrades made a run for it, "I don't want them to think I'm just some nut who escaped from the loony bin. I thought you were going to introduce me. You know, tell them I'm not certifiable."

My friend looked at me like I really had escaped from a rubber room. "I don't want to lose my job, Hilde. In case these people go ballistic. . ."

I jumped to my feet. "Hold on. Do you really think they'll react that badly? Maybe you could just hand them a note. . . ."

Paula laughed. "Oh, that would be good. 'Here grieving family. Someone left an anonymous note for you. They think you just eulogized a stranger. Have a nice day!' I don't think so."

A feeling of panic began to wiggle around in my brain. This approach had sounded good in my head, but putting it into practice was proving to be something else altogether. "Maybe this isn't such a good idea."

Paula came up and put her arms around me. "Listen sweetie, you're doing the right thing. Just introduce yourself, tell them you did the phony Mabel's hair, and explain what happened. Tell them you're not completely sure the bodies were switched, but you felt you had to be honest about what you saw. Trust me, they won't be upset with you. If they get mad at all, it will be with Druther's. You don't need to worry."

"Maybe," I said glumly. "Most of the time when people

tell me I don't need to worry, it's time to start worrying."

Paula stepped back and grinned at me. "I thought you said worrying was an insult to God. That when you worry, you're not trusting Him." She laughed at my startled expression. "See, I do listen, even though I don't buy everything you say."

I lightly punched her on the arm. "Oh, great. So the only reason you pay attention is so you can throw it back in my face. Lovely."

Paula gave me another quick hug. "You know one thing I respect about you? You always try to do the right thing. There aren't too many people out there like that."

Her comment should have made me feel good, but since at that very moment I was looking with interest at the easiest way out instead of the right way out, it only brought conviction.

"Okay, get going. I'll be in the foyer when the service is over. No matter what, I'm going to talk to them. God help me."

Paula patted my shoulder. "If He's who you say He is, I'm sure He will. See you afterwards."

She walked out of the office, pulling the door shut behind her. I sat down on the couch again and thought about what she'd said. Usually Paula only mentioned God in a negative way. Today's comments were different. Was it a sign that she was beginning to listen? I'd prayed diligently for her for quite some time, but I didn't have any faith in my own ability to lead her to God. I'd learned that I can't do the Holy Spirit's job—opening hearts and minds and drawing people to Jesus. My part is to pray and believe that God hears my prayers. Sometimes answers come quickly. Sometimes it takes longer. But they always come. I took a minute to thank Him for loving Paula and preparing her heart for Him. Then I asked Him to give me the right words to say to Mabel's family. I looked up at the clock. Time to get to the foyer. Hopefully I would soon be saying good-bye to Mabel.

I got up and opened the door. No one was in the hallway. I quietly walked toward the chapel. The service was still going. Although the doors were shut, I could hear a man speaking. It had to be Alfred Winnemaker. After a few minutes he stopped. An organ began to play "Amazing Grace," and several voices joined in. After the fourth verse, the organ switched to a slow dirge. This signaled the end of the service. The door to the chapel swung open, and one of Willowbrook's staff members secured it. Then he opened the other door and fastened it also. He took his place next to the door so he could greet each person as they left.

I glanced quickly into the chapel. A few people walked toward the doors. A couple stood up at the front, next to the coffin. That had to be Alfred and Edith. I smiled at the folks who exited past me. Everyone finally filtered out except the Winnemakers. It was obvious that saying good-bye was difficult for them. Little did they know I was waiting in the wings to make it worse. If I could have made a quick getaway,

I would have. But I had no choice. I had to tell them the truth. Mabel deserved it, and so did the family of the poor woman lying in that casket. Finally the Winnemakers turned and started walking down the aisle toward me. Alfred and Edith were probably in their late fifties or early sixties. They moved slowly, like people whose health wasn't good. Edith wiped her eyes with her hankie while she leaned against Alfred, although I wasn't sure who was supporting whom. I glanced around, but Paula had already disappeared. I probably wasn't going to see her again anytime soon.

Edith noticed me standing near the door and gave me a tremulous smile. She had a sweet face framed with soft, grayish hair. "Do you work for Willowbrook, dear?" she said in a melodious, high-pitched voice.

"No, ma'am," I said. "I—I need to talk to you a minute. It's about your aunt."

They stopped in front of me, looks of puzzlement on their faces. "I don't recognize you," Alfred said. "How did you know Aunt Mabel?"

I pointed to a couch that sat against the wall. "Can we sit down for a minute? I'd like to explain, if you'll let me."

"Why, certainly, dear," Edith said. "We're not in any hurry, are we, Papa?"

Alfred, a rather round, balding man, smiled and patted his wife's shoulder. "We do need to get a little food into Mama before too long—it's her blood sugar you know. But I never turn down requests from pretty girls, do I, Mama?"

Edith playfully slapped his arm. "You'd better settle down." She took my arm as we made our way to the couch. "You'll have to excuse my husband. He's incorrigible."

The couple took seats on the floral upholstered couch. I sat in a russet-colored wing-back chair next to them. The muted lights in the foyer and the color-coordinated seating next to the dark wood paneling on the walls gave off somber but relaxing vibes. A nearby wall fountain provided a soothing sound as water trickled down the front and splashed into the bowl at the bottom. Everything was geared to provide a peaceful place for family members to talk and commiserate about the passing of someone important in their lives. My guess was, however, that very few people had gathered together to hear what I was getting ready to say.

The Winnemakers scooted around a little until they were comfortable. Then they both fastened their eyes on me expectantly.

This was it. I launched another silent prayer, took a big gulp of air, and began. "Mr. and Mrs. Winnemaker, I have something I must tell you. My intention is not to upset you, but something happened concerning your aunt that I feel compelled to share with you."

"My goodness, dear. What is it?" Edith had grabbed her husband's arm. "I can't think of anything you could possibly say that would upset us. I mean, our beloved Mabel is dead. What could you tell us that would make things worse?"

"You—you see, it was my job to style Mabel's hair. Even

though you asked for a closed casket, we wanted to make her look as nice as possible in case you or another family member changed your minds. Do you understand?"

Alfred nodded and patted his wife's arm. "Of course we do. And that's exactly what we wanted. Just in case William, that's her grandson, made it into the country in time for the funeral. Is there some kind of problem?"

"It's about Mabel. She. . ." But before I could get my next words out, a strong hand gripped my shoulder. I yelped in pain and looked up into the furious face of Ron Druther.

"Would you please excuse us, Mr. and Mrs. Winnemaker?" he said between clenched teeth. "Miss Higgins and I need a word." With that, he pulled me to my feet and pushed me none too gently toward the empty chapel, but not before telling Alfred and Edith that they should go home and get some rest. I didn't get the chance to find out if they heeded his advice or not. He pulled the chapel doors shut behind him, and I couldn't see the Winnemakers—or anything else, except for Ron's livid features. The lights had been turned down in the chapel, giving it an eerie ambience. This wasn't where I wanted to be right now, and I didn't like being manhandled. This was the second time Ron had gotten overly physical with me.

"What in the world are you thinking, Miss Higgins?" he said in a tone seething with rage. "These people just lost their aunt. Her remains have been all but incinerated. Now you want to upset them with this ridiculous story about bodies being switched? What is wrong with you, young lady? Are you demented?"

I stepped quickly around to the other side of a nearby pew, putting some space between the enraged man and myself. My shoulder hurt where he'd grabbed it. "Why are you here?" I asked. "This isn't your service anymore."

He leaned over, his face inches from mine. "Of course it's still my service. Thanks to the fire, we moved it to this location, but I'm still overseeing things. And I won't have you causing distress to those two grieving people. For the last time, that's Mabel Winnemaker in that coffin. Leave this alone!" He suddenly slumped back, almost falling into the pew behind him. His expression crumbled. Even in the muted light I could see tears in his eyes. I wanted to feel sorry for him, but I was still too upset about being pushed around.

"I can't leave them alone," I hissed at him. "That is *not* Mabel Winnemaker. You must know it, too. Is that why you burned down your own funeral home? To cover your tracks? Or was it for the insurance money?"

His jaw dropped as he stared back at me. Then for some reason he started to laugh, making him seem slightly unhinged. I realized for the first time that I might be in actual danger. I was gauging the distance to the nearest door and whether or not I could make it without being tackled by this insane funeral director, when Ron finally grew quiet.

"Hilde," he said, after taking a deep breath, "you truly don't know what you're talking about. Why would I destroy my only source of income to cover something that only exists in your imagination? There was no mistake made with Mabel Winnemaker. You admitted there weren't any other women waiting for services while she was with us. That makes your whole premise impossible. Besides, I would never, ever endanger Gwen Cox." He sighed. "The truth is, I loved her. I'd hoped we'd end up together someday. It's been five years since my wife died. I never thought I'd fall in love again, but I did. Unfortunately, I wasn't her type. And besides the fact that I would never do anything that might hurt her," he started to chuckle again, "your whole conjecture about how I would somehow profit from a fire is the most ludicrous thing of all." He wiped away the tears that had streaked down his face. "You see, because of some recent financial setbacks, I let my property insurance lapse." He shook his head. "I've lost everything, you silly girl. There's no insurance. No way to make it right. And no way to start again." He grinned at me, his eyes wild. "Kind of rips a big hole in your conspiracy theory, doesn't it?"

I was flabbergasted. And deflated. Why *would* Ron burn down his funeral home if he knew there was no insurance? It didn't make sense. I quit thinking about making a run for it. The man in front of me was obviously defeated. The bluster was gone.

"Mr. Druther," I said as soothingly as possible, "I'm sorry for you. I really am. If I misjudged you, I apologize. But that is not Mabel Winnemaker in that casket. Her family needs to know the truth. And someone needs to find the real Mabel's body and identify this other poor woman. It's the right thing to do. Can't you see that?"

Ron shook his head slowly. "The only thing I have left is my reputation. If you spread this absurd story, I'll lose that, too."

"I'll do what I can to keep that from happening," I said quietly. "But the truth is the truth, and it must be told."

He'd just opened up his mouth to say something else, when the doors to the chapel swung open.

"Hilde? Hilde, are you in here?"

Paula. Thank God. I stood up and called out, "Here I am."

She switched on the lights and looked surprised to see Ron sitting next to me. "Are you okay?" she asked with alarm.

Ron pulled himself up. "She's fine. I'm not the monster you think I am. I wouldn't hurt her—or anyone else." He walked slowly toward the doorway, turning around just before he disappeared through the doors. "You do whatever you have to do, Miss Higgins. I don't care anymore."

Paula watched him leave. "What was that all about?" she asked.

"I—I don't know." I frowned at my friend. "Ron let his property insurance expire. He's not covered for the fire."

"Wow." Paula shook her head. "He's in big trouble then. Not only is he out of business, but I wouldn't be surprised to see some lawsuits over the bodies that were lost."

"I doubt seriously that he set that fire, Paula. And I'm pretty sure he didn't kill Gwen. He was in love with her."

"So where does that leave you?"

I walked quickly toward the chapel doors and looked into the foyer. The Winnemakers were gone. "Right back where I started," I said with a sigh. "Now I'll have to go to their home. Good thing I have a photographic memory."

Paula waved her hand at me. "Don't let them think I gave you their address. I could get in a lot of trouble."

"They're probably in the phone book anyway. I doubt anyone will think you had anything to do with it." I reached over and gave her a hug. "Thanks for trying to help me. Maybe it didn't turn out the way we thought it would, but at least I know more than I did. I'd hoped this would be the end of the road for Mabel and me, but our journey doesn't seem quite finished." I pointed toward the casket at the front of the room. "What happens now?"

"Cremation. It's pretty close to that already. We just have to finish the process."

"Makes sense, I guess."

Paula closed the chapel doors behind us. "Gus ought to be back soon. You probably better get out of here. I'd rather not explain your presence."

"I left my purse in your office. Let me grab it, and I'll take off."

I followed her back to her office and found my purse. "Any plans tonight?" I asked, before I remembered she'd just broken up with her latest boyfriend. Friday night was usually a big night for Paula. To my surprise, she grinned.

"As a matter of fact, I have a date." She clapped her hands together. "A guy who works for a local mortuary service finally asked me out. I've flirted with him for a long time. I can't believe I finally got through to him. We're going to the Beach Club."

I was glad to see the delighted look on her face. I leaned over and kissed her on the cheek. "I hope you have a wonderful time, but stay away from a waiter named Clive."

She laughed. "I'll do my best. You have any plans for tonight?"

I chuckled. "Yes. I have a date, too. He's around seventy years old. I'm cooking dinner for him."

"Uh-oh. I assume SPAM® products will be involved?"

I put my hand on the doorknob and swung it open. Before I stepped outside, I turned and grinned at her. "Oh, SPAM® products will *definitely* be involved."

I closed the door and jogged quickly to my car, hoping to get away before Gus returned. A sharp winter wind lashed against my face, and dark, heavy clouds gathered overhead. Another blanket of snow would make my trip home rather precarious, but there was no way I could postpone my meeting with the Winnemakers. It felt cruel to bother them so soon after the service, yet I felt that time was of the essence. Mabel's grandson would be in Wichita in a couple of days. Better that a family member explain this bizarre situation than for a stranger to drop a bombshell in his lap.

In my mind, I pulled up the page I'd seen in Gwen's file

the day I went to work on Mabel. The picture was as clear as it had been that day. I saw the Winnemakers' address: 826 N. Livingston. I also saw the phone number. I'd known someone in school who lived on Livingston, so I knew where it was and headed that way. When I was a few blocks away, I pulled over and rummaged in my purse for my cell phone. As usual, it was on the bottom. As I pulled it out, a bright green pen came with it and landed on the passenger seat of my car. I picked it up. Erma's House of Pancakes and Puppies – Little River, Tennessee. For crying out loud. I'd never been to Tennessee in my life. I tossed it back in my purse with a vow to clean it out the first chance I got. I punched in Alfred and Edith's telephone number and waited. Someone picked it up on the third ring.

"Hello?"

It was Edith's sweet, soft voice. I steeled myself and said, "Mrs. Winnemaker? This is Hilde Higgins. I met you at the funeral home? I'm sorry you had to leave before I had a chance to speak with you. I wonder, would it be possible for me to stop by your house and talk to you for a few minutes? I promise I won't stay long."

"Why of course you may, my dear. I apologize for our hasty retreat. I needed to eat a little something and take my shot—diabetes, you know. But we're here now, and we'd love to have you stop by. Do you have our address?"

I told her I did and that I was only a short distance away. With a promise to wait just a little bit so she could "tidy up,"

I drove over to the street where they lived. It was an older part of town, but the houses were well kept and the neighborhood was pleasant. I parked for about fifteen minutes and then pulled up into the driveway of 826, behind an old station wagon. I got out of the car and knocked on the door. Alfred answered it with a smile.

"Please come in. I'm sorry, tell me your name one more time. Mama and I are getting a little forgetful."

I introduced myself again and was escorted to an attractive overstuffed chair in a living room that was sparsely furnished yet cozy and comfortable. A small fire burned in the redbrick fireplace. The wallpaper sported small red roses. It was faded, as was the furniture. But everything was "clean as a whistle and neat as a pin," as my mother used to say when she'd tell me to clean my room. I hated that phrase, but I had to admit that it applied to the Winnemakers' home.

Edith toddled in. "So nice to see you again, dear. How about a cup of coffee?"

"I'd love one, thanks."

Alfred sat down on a rust-colored couch that had seen better days. Lace doilies on the arms and a patchwork quilt on the back were probably used to hide worn spots. It was obvious from the seat cushions that a lot of sitting had been done there.

Not wanting to launch into my reason for inviting myself over without a warm-up, I waited until Edith returned with my coffee then smiled at the couple who sat expectantly on the couch, waiting for me to tell them why I was stalking them. "So Mabel lived here with you?" I asked.

"Yes," Alfred said, tears filling his eyes. "You see, when we found out she was ailing and alone, we offered to move here and take care of her. Her grandson, William, a wonderful young man, had been offered a job overseas."

"But he wouldn't take it because he didn't want to leave Mabel alone," Edith said, interrupting her husband. She reached over and took his hand. "We just couldn't allow William to do that. He's young and has his whole life ahead of him. We're getting older, and besides, we felt like it was our duty to do what we could. We left our home in Arizona and came here, even though this climate is a little hard on our arthritis."

"I'd hurt my back in a fall and couldn't work much," Alfred said. "So it turned out good for everyone. William has been very generous to us, giving us money every month to care for his grandmother. And he paid for this house. You see, Mabel's house was too small for all of us."

"We were a very happy family," Edith said with a catch in her voice. She reached into her dress pocket, pulled out a lace handkerchief, and wiped her brimming eyes. "I'm sorry, dear. I'm afraid I've been a very weepy old woman today. I must admit now that Mabel is gone, Alfred and I are a little concerned about what we're going to do. The house was in Mabel's name, and of course there won't be any more money from William to care for his grandmother." A small sob escaped her lips. She wiped her eyes again. "Oh dear. You must think I'm very selfish to be thinking about our future on the day we said good-bye to our sweet, sweet Mabel. I don't mean to appear so coldhearted."

I could feel my own eyes getting moist. These poor people had lost someone dear to them and were wondering if they were going to end up on the street. Now I was getting ready to make everything worse. "I don't think you're coldhearted at all," I said as gently as I could. "You've been through a great deal. Wondering what will happen next is only natural."

"Well, thank you, young lady, for saying that," Alfred said. "You're a very encouraging person. I'm glad you came to see us today, but you're allowing us to use up all your time. You wanted to talk to us about something. What was it?"

I cleared my throat and was trying to find the right words when I noticed a yellow ball stuck under one corner of the couch. "Mabel's dog," I blurted out. "Where is he?"

Edith raised one eyebrow and stared at me. "Her dog? You came all the way over here about her dog? Oh, my."

Alfred shook his head slowly. "I'm so sorry, dear. We couldn't keep the dog. We have no idea where we will live, and treating his asthma is just too expensive for us. We took him to the shelter. But not to worry. He's a pug, you know. People love them. I'm sure he'll be adopted."

Edith nodded with enthusiasm. "Yes. He's only eight years old. He'll make someone a wonderful pet."

My heart dropped to my toes. An eight-year-old dog

with asthma? No one in their right mind was going to adopt that dog.

"If you want him, he might still be at the shelter," Alfred said. "But you'd better hurry. No way to know how long he'll last."

I nodded dumbly. Mabel's beloved dog. He was probably days away from joining his mistress.

"Is that all you wanted?" Edith asked. "I don't know why you thought we would be upset. Papa and I would be thrilled if you took Watson. I wish we'd known you wanted him before we took him down there." She shook her head. "I'm afraid there might be a fee to get him out, dear. I'm so sorry. . . ."

"No," I said, interrupting her. "That's—that's not why I came."

Alfred made a sweeping motion with his hand. "I'm sorry. Mama and I jump to conclusions sometimes. Please. Go ahead and talk. We'll be quiet and put on our listening ears."

Both of them held their cupped hands next to their ears and smiled at me. I felt like someone who'd just walked into a senior center with a stick of dynamite in one hand and a lighter in the other. The only thing left was to ignite it and throw it in their laps. I reminded myself that I had no choice. "It's about Mabel. As I told you at the funeral home, I was called in to style her hair."

"Yes," Edith said, her head bobbing up and down. "We

sent over a picture so you would know how she wore it." She paused for a moment. "That's how you knew about her dog, isn't it? From her picture."

"Sorry we couldn't come up with something better," Alfred said with a sigh, "but Mabel had already sent William almost every picture she had. She knew she didn't have long, poor dear. She only kept the picture we gave you because Watson was in it."

So that was it. Now it made sense. "It would have worked out just fine," I said tentatively, "except."—I took a deep breath—"the person I was asked to work on wasn't your aunt. It wasn't Mabel."

It was like a bucket of cold water had been thrown on both of them. Edith's mouth dropped open, and Alfred's skin tone turned even pastier.

"You see," I continued. "I saw Mabel before she was sent to the coroner's office. Her hair was soft and had exactly the kind of natural part I saw in her picture. But when I went back the second time, the hair was different. Completely different. I'm certain it wasn't the same woman."

The expression on Alfred's face concerned me. It reminded me of the way Gabe looked when I'd delivered his package.

"I'm—I'm sorry, young lady—Hilde, but I think you must be wrong. Where would Mabel be if she wasn't in that coffin? I—I don't understand." Edith began to weep softly.

I felt bad. Really bad. "Look," I said, "if I could have kept this to myself, I would have. The last thing I want to do is upset you two. But Mabel is still out there somewhere. I mean, her body is out there somewhere. And the family of the other woman has the right to know where she is."

"We understand, dear," Edith said. "We really do. This has all been so trying. . . ."

"Did you tell the funeral home about your suspicions?" Alfred asked, his voice a little stronger than before. "What did they say?"

"Yes, I told them, but they didn't believe me." I looked back and forth between the obviously shell-shocked couple. "I had no other choice but to bring this to you. You can do whatever you feel you need to with the information. It's entirely up to you." I reached into my purse and pulled out one of my business cards. "All my contact information is on my card. If I can do anything to help you, all you have to do is let me know. I don't intend to pursue this any further. I've really done all I can."

I stood up and handed my card to Alfred. "So it's up to us?" Alfred said. "You don't want to be involved?"

I nodded. "That's right. No more interference. There are several people who are very unhappy with me about this situation. And it's really your business, not mine. But if you need me. . ."

Alfred handed my card to Edith and stood up. "Please understand that what you've shared is quite shocking to us. We'll certainly follow up. To be honest with you, William is much more knowledgeable about things like this. When he arrives, we'll tell him about your concerns. If anyone can get to the bottom of this, he can."

I reached out and shook Alfred's hand. "I'm so relieved. I—I just want what's best for you and for your aunt's memory. There could very well be another family who is confused and hurting as well. I hope this mix-up is finally resolved in a way that will bring you some peace. I'm very sorry for your loss."

Alfred pumped my hand a few times, his eyes still teary. "My aunt was a wonderful woman, my dear. You would have loved her as we did."

Edith got up and shuffled over to me. "What a heavy burden you've had to carry," she said, her eyes full of compassion. "I am so sorry you were put in such an awful position." She wrapped her arms around me and gave me a hug. She smelled like lilacs. My grandmother had smelled the same way. I fought back my own tears.

"Thank you," I said. "You're very kind and understanding."

Edith stepped back and patted me on the shoulder. "Now you go on home, and don't worry about this anymore. We'll take care of everything."

I nodded and had started for the door when that silly yellow ball caught my eye again. Something they'd said popped into my brain. "What—what did you say Mabel's dog was named?"

"Watson, dear," Edith said. "Mabel loved to read. She started out every morning reading her Bible. She was quite religious, you know. After that, the rest of the day was spent in her favorite mystery novel. She adored Sherlock Holmes, although she also read tons of Agatha Christie." She clapped her hands together. "I don't suppose you're a fan of Holmes as well?"

Mabel liked Agatha Christie and Sherlock Holmes. I was beginning to feel very connected to a woman I would never get to meet on this side of heaven. "Yes," I said softly. "I'm a great fan."

Edith toddled over to a built-in bookshelf near the fireplace. "Just a minute, dear," she said. "Now where is that . . ." She pulled a large book off the shelf. "Here it is." She came over to where I stood by the door. "I want you to have this. It was her very favorite book. She read it and reread it."

I looked down at the cover: *The Return of Sherlock Holmes.* The title was in gold against a dark green background. "I don't have this one," I said. "These are the stories written after Arthur Conan Doyle tried to get rid of Sherlock by having him die in Reichenbach Falls with Professor Moriarty."

A look at her blank expression told me that she had no earthly idea what I was talking about, and if I continued, she and her husband would probably decide I really was batty. I smiled reassuringly. "Sorry. I'm just such a big Sherlock Holmes fan, I tend to go on and on when someone gives me an opportunity." I took the book from her hand. "Thank you so much. I'll treasure this."

"You're very welcome," Edith said. Her expression still showed a slight concern for my mental stability, but I was fairly certain I was back on firm ground. I waved good-bye to Alfred, who smiled and returned the gesture. I beat a hasty retreat to my car, relieved to finally be rid of my Mabel problem. But for some reason the face of that silly dog in the photo with Mabel kept running through my mind. A photographic memory can be a blessing when you want to remember something, but when you need to forget, the mind has a will of its own.

On the way to the store, my stomach began to rumble with hunger. I pulled into a drive-in fast-food restaurant. At that moment, anything that wouldn't run away from me seemed appetizing. I'd just ordered a foot-long cheese coney and tater tots when my phone rang. It was Paula.

I clicked the SEND button and said, "Hello?"

"Hilde," Paula hissed through the phone. "Gus got back right after you left. I had to tell him about your run-in with Ron Druther. I figured Ron would bring it up, and I wanted to tell Gus first."

It hadn't occurred to me that Paula would tell Gus about our encounter. I hoped she wouldn't get in any trouble. "Did he get mad?"

"A little," she said, her voice so low I could barely hear her. It was obvious she didn't want to be overheard. "But that's not why I'm calling you."

I sighed. I was emotionally drained after my meeting with the Winnemakers, and I wasn't in the mood to play games. "What's going on, Paula? I'm getting ready to eat lunch."

"Gus told me that Ron lost most of his money in the stock market. And guess who his stockbroker is?"

I felt my body go cold from more than the frigid temperatures outside. Before I could answer her, she said, "Adam Sawyer. Isn't that the guy you told me about? Maybe you already knew this. But if he didn't tell you about it himself, it seems more than a little odd to me."

I thanked her and turned off my phone. It seemed more than a little odd to me, too. Why hadn't Adam told me Ron was his client? Possibilities flooded my mind. And none of them were good.

CHAPTER ⫙⫙⫙ TEN

It was twenty minutes till six when I popped my SPAM® Classic stuffed zucchinis into the oven. I'd just taken my cheese and garlic biscuits out and wrapped them in tinfoil to keep them warm when the microwave dinged, announcing the corn was ready. I took out the container, covered it, and placed it inside my picnic basket.

It had been a strange day. First the odd picture I'd seen at Gabe's. Then my encounters with the Winnemakers and Ron Druther. Finally the revelation that Adam not only knew Ron Druther, he was fully aware of Ron's money problems. I couldn't understand it. Maybe Gus was mistaken. Maybe Ron's stockbroker only worked at Adam's firm. I'd almost convinced myself that it was a simple mistake by the time I took the zucchini out of the oven. They were beautifully toasted, and the cheese on top had melted perfectly. The heavenly aroma filled my little kitchen, and my stomach rumbled with hunger. I'd been so upset by Paula's call that I'd barely nibbled on my lunch.

I'd just gotten everything packed and ready to go when there was a knock on my door. Since I almost never had visitors, it took me by surprise. I opened the door to find Mrs. Hudson standing there.

"I'm sorry to bother you, Hilde," she whispered. "But I must speak to you about a very serious matter."

I glanced at my watch. Ten till six. "I–I'm kind of in a hurry, Mrs. Hudson. I'm expected at Mr. Bashevis's at six."

Her eyebrows and her volume got higher. "Gabriel Bashevis?"

I nodded.

"Why, Hilde Higgins. You made friends with that old goat?" She offered me a quick smile. "Good for you. I've tried to get to know him for twenty years. He's never so much as given me the time of day."

I was happy she was so impressed with my social skills, but I wanted to serve dinner while it was still hot. "I'm sorry, Mrs. Hudson, but you said you wanted to talk to me about something?"

"Oh, yes. Goodness, I almost forgot." She stepped forward and would have run into me if I hadn't moved out of the way. Reluctantly, I let her into the apartment and closed the door behind her.

"Maybe I should call Gabe and tell him I'll be a little late," I said, hoping she would take the hint.

Instead she made a clicking sound with her teeth and frowned at me. "Gabe, is it? Now Hilde, you must remember that even though he seems old to you, Mr. Bashevis is still a man. You need to be careful, you know. Why I can't tell you the number of times I. . ."

"Mrs. Hudson," I said as politely as I could while interrupting her, "I assure you that Gabe is a perfect gentleman. We're only friends." The idea of something more with Gabe Bashevis made me want to giggle, but suddenly the picture of him when he was younger flashed in my mind. I felt my face flush. "What was it you wanted to tell me? My food is going to get cold. . . ."

"I apologize, dear." Every time Mrs. Hudson visited, her eyes darted around my room. She was probably looking to see if I was doing anything that would permanently ruin the place for future tenants. She finally seemed satisfied that I hadn't built a fire pit in the middle of the floor or painted murals of sea monkeys on the walls. "I'm afraid we have a rather serious problem on our hands, Hilde," she said pointedly. "We have a thief in the house."

Although I wasn't surprised by her comment since I'd overheard her and Minnie talking about it, I tried to look shocked. "How awful. What's been stolen?"

She shook her head sadly. "Minnie and I have both had money taken from our purses. Some of my jewelry is missing, and a valuable lamp that belonged to my grandmother has disappeared. Oh, and Mr. Sims *says* his gold pocket watch is gone, along with his wife's wedding ring."

"But you don't believe him?"

She raised her eyebrows in disdain. "I'm sorry to say I don't. He seems very suspicious to me. Where does he go every day? He hardly speaks to anyone." She lowered her voice to almost a whisper. "I trust you, Hilde, and I know Minnie is above suspicion. So who else could it be?"

I wanted to tell her my first choice would be Derek, but I didn't have time to get into it. "I have no idea, but I like Mr. Sims. Besides, how could it be him? He's gone every day, and you're home almost every night."

"I can't see well at night," she said. "I try to run all my errands while the sun's out."

"That's my point," I said, trying to keep the irritation out of my voice. "Just when would he have pulled off all these robberies?"

Her face wrinkled in a frown. She looked like a basset hound with a problem. "I hadn't really thought about it like that."

"Besides, you said someone broke into his apartment and took some jewelry."

"Well, that could just be a cover. . . ."

I almost laughed. Mrs. Hudson's detective skills left a lot to be desired. "You know, so far the only person who hasn't been robbed is me. Maybe I'm the thief."

She wagged her chubby finger at me. "That's not funny, Hilde. I trust you. Besides, what in the world would anyone want in here?"

I probably should have been offended, but she was right.

I glanced at my watch again. Six o'clock. Great. I reached around Mrs. Hudson and opened the door. "I'm sorry to run off like this, but I really must go. Maybe we could talk about it more tomorrow."

She nodded absentmindedly. "Certainly, dear. Tomorrow." With that, she started to walk out. Then she stopped. "Oh, I almost forgot. I mixed up a brand-new tea today. That darling Derek bought me the most wonderful herbs." She smiled and put her hand to her chest. "I'm afraid I ruined his surprise by accidentally finding them when I put clean sheets on his bed, but he forgave me. I was so touched that he thought of me. This is a very special brew. Let me know what you think of it." She reached into her apron pocket and pulled out one of her dreadful plastic bags. I took it and thanked her. She smiled and left. I could hear her orthopedic shoes clumping down the wooden stairs.

I grabbed my basket, stuck the new stinky tea in my purse, and waved good-bye to Sherlock. On the way to my car, I glanced over at the basement windows. The lights were off, which meant Derek was probably gone. I intended to keep an eye on him. Taking Mr. Sims's dead wife's wedding ring was below contempt. Someone would probably have to catch him in the act for Mrs. Hudson to believe that "darling Derek" was robbing her blind.

It was just a few minutes after six when I turned the knob on Gabe's front door. I was surprised when he pulled it open himself.

"Sorry," I said. "Mrs. Hudson corralled me in my apartment. I guess someone in the house is stealing. It's getting pretty bad."

He closed the door behind me. "Sorry to hear that," he said with a frown. "Have you lost anything?" He took the basket from my hands and pointed toward the stairs. I took off my coat and tossed it on the bear, then I obediently headed that way.

"No. Not that I know of. Of course, I don't have anything valuable—except the music box you gave me. I'm afraid some of the things that were stolen were important keepsakes."

I followed Gabe into the dining room. The table was set with china that matched the teacups he'd used the first time I'd been invited to his apartment. There were ivory linen napkins next to our plates, and the silverware had gold handles that went perfectly with the china. Crystal goblets filled with water were next to the dishes, and a silver coffee pitcher sat in the middle of the table.

"Goodness," I said, "I'm not sure my simple dinner is worth all this. If I'd known you planned to be this fancy, I'd have fixed prime rib or something."

Gabe grunted. "I just thought it would be nice to eat in the dining room one night."

I smiled. "Thanks. It is nice. And you set a beautiful table."

"Don't be silly. You're making too big a deal out of it. Now tell me what you've prepared for us this evening."

I'd just started to take the food out of the basket when a soft alarm sounded. "What's that?" I asked, startled. Was it a fire alarm? Was this tinderbox about ready to go up?

"Someone's at the door," Gabe said casually. He walked over to a small rolltop desk that sat in an alcove in the living room. He slid the desk open. Surprisingly, there was a video screen inside. Although I couldn't see the screen clearly from where I was, I could tell that whoever was standing at the front door was visible. Gabe had installed a surveillance camera at the entrance to his store. Why in the world would he need video surveillance? As if reading my mind, he closed the desktop and turned to me. "I don't like to sit in the store all day. This way I can stay upstairs and only go down when I have a customer."

I nodded at him. It made sense, but it still seemed odd to me. I wondered how many times he'd watched me when I didn't know it. The idea creeped me out a little.

"Excuse me," he said. "I'll be right back."

I'd just finished putting the food on the table and sticking a slotted serving spoon in the corn when I heard him coming up the stairs. I looked over, expecting to see Gabe. Instead, Adam stuck his head around the corner and grinned at me.

"Adam!" He was the last person I'd expected to see. My first reaction was a small tremor of delight—but then I remembered the news about Ron Druther. My happiness was chased away by a burst of suspicion. "What are you doing here?"

He walked slowly into the living room, his eyes drawn to the opulent surroundings. His expression reminded me of the first time I'd ventured into Gabe's living quarters. They were a startling change from the shabby surroundings downstairs. I gave him a moment to recover. Finally, he looked at me.

"What are you doing here, Adam?" I repeated. My tone sounded almost accusatory. I hadn't meant it to.

His eyebrows arched in surprise. "I—I just wanted to make sure you were okay. I tried calling, but you didn't answer your phone. Your landlady told me you were here."

I offered him a slight smile, hoping to soften the effect of my earlier reaction. "Oh. Thank you. It's been a long day, but I'm okay."

"Has something happened?" Gabe asked, coming into the room.

I nodded. "I haven't had a chance to tell you, but things have taken a rather odd turn."

"Sounds intriguing, but let's talk after we eat. I would hate to see your wonderful food get cold." Gabe looked at Adam. "We were just sitting down to eat dinner. Why don't you join us?"

I wasn't sure I wanted Adam to stay, but this was Gabe's home, he'd just taken the choice out of my hands. Frankly, his quick acceptance of Adam surprised me. It had taken him awhile to warm up to me, and Mrs. Hudson still hadn't fallen under his good graces. I stared at him questioningly, but all I got back was a blank look.

"If—if you're sure I'm not intruding. . ."

Adam's comment was made more to me than to Gabe. I smiled reassuringly. "I'm Gabe's guest. If it's all right with him. . ."

"I haven't hosted a dinner party in ages," the old man said with a chuckle. "I would enjoy the company. After dinner, you can bring me up to snuff on your situation, Hilde. Excuse me a minute while I get your young man a plate and some silverware."

I watched him shuffle toward the kitchen. Who would have thought that Gabriel Bashevis could be such a gracious host? It was nice—and a little fishy. But frankly, I was tired of being suspicious about everything and everyone. Now that the situation with Mabel was out of my life, maybe I could finally relax a little. However, there were still some nagging questions that needed to be answered. Like why Adam hadn't told me about Ron.

Gabe brought in another place setting, and we sat down to eat. Gabe said the blessing over the food and complimented me on how good everything looked.

"Stuffed zucchini!" Adam said with a wide smile. "Love it. And these rolls look incredible. Why, Hilde. You're a woman of many talents."

I laughed. "I wouldn't count them. I'm afraid you'd have a hard time using all the fingers of one hand. I do like to cook though. In fact, I even enter a recipe at the state fair every year."

Adam swallowed a large mouthful of my main dish. "Delicious!" he exclaimed. "That's the best stuffed zucchini I've ever tasted."

"Yes, it's quite good," Gabe said. "It reminds me of a similar dish I used to eat in Hawaii." The twinkle in his eye told me he already knew my secret ingredient. Most people don't figure it out before I tell them.

"You should enter this dish in a contest," Adam mumbled. "It's heavenly."

"I did, actually," I said with a smile. "I won second place."

"That's incredible for a main dish competition. Or was it under the vegetable category?"

Gabe chuckled. "I would guess it was entered under the SPAM® category."

Adam looked puzzled. "Spam? Like bad e-mail?"

Gabe grinned at him. "No, dear boy. SPAM®—as in the meat product."

Adam's eyes got big. I wasn't sure if he was going to laugh or cry. "This is SPAM®? Are you serious?" He stared down at his plate like a bug had crawled there and died. Then he started to laugh. "SPAM®. Hilde, you're the only person I know who could get me to eat SPAM®." He shook his head. "You know what? I can't believe what I've been missing. This is delicious. Do you have any other recipes like this?"

I nodded. "You bet. I love it. I've entered the contest at the fair the last two years. I'm working on a new recipe for next year. I intend to win this time."

"You know, Adam," Gabe said, "SPAM® products are incredibly popular in Hawaii. They've gotten some hard knocks here on the mainland, but it isn't deserved. I happen to enjoy them myself."

Adam shook his head slowly. "Well. I guess my borders have been increased a little tonight." He smiled at me and held out his plate. "Can I have another stuffed zucchini, please?"

I put one on his plate. Gabe held his plate out as well, and I served him. Good thing I'd prepared plenty.

We made small talk while we finished dinner. Gabe asked Adam several general questions about his work and his family. Adam told him stories from our childhood—thankfully, he left out the nude showering.

At one point during our discussion, my eyes strayed to the painting of the woman with the haunted eyes. I thought back to the picture I'd seen in Gabe's secret package. What had happened to change her countenance so drastically? The joy I'd seen in her photograph was gone—replaced with a kind of profound sadness. I must have stared at the portrait a little too long, because I caught Gabe looking at me with an odd expression on his face. I smiled and jumped back into the conversation, hoping he wouldn't think my interest was unusual.

When we were finished, Gabe cleared the dishes, insisting that Adam and I go into the living room and wait for tea and dessert. After one more attempt to offer our help, we gave up and settled down on Gabe's soft leather couch, where we watched the flames dance in the white-stone fireplace.

"I called a client who's connected to the fire department," Adam said when we were comfortably seated. "He confirmed that they're handling the fire as 'suspicious.' However, that doesn't mean it was arson. It will take some time for them to make a final determination. As I told you, the fire started in the back, near some highly flammable materials. The building was old with lots of wood. That's why there was so much damage. A lot of the newer mortuaries are made of concrete or brick and designed to be fireproof."

"I understand all of that," I said slowly. "But I still can't figure out why Gwen was in the back of the building. I've considered your idea that she might have been trying to put out the fire, but I don't think she'd do that. She'd stay in her office and call for help. Then I think she'd get out of there. I mean, it's not like there was anyone she had to save."

Adam shrugged. "Maybe she was locking up? Seems she was the last one there."

"Maybe." I thought about it for a moment. "The only doors I can think of that might need to be secured lead to the alley. They're used for pickups and deliveries, but they're kept locked when they're not being used. Unless they found another body in the back that someone had dropped off. . ."

"My client didn't mention that."

"Then that explanation doesn't seem plausible."

Adam scooted a little closer to me and stared into the fireplace. "You may have to accept the fact that you might never know what really happened, Hilde. The only person who could tell us is gone."

"Maybe. But if someone set that fire. . ."

Adam grunted then turned to frown at me. "Don't you have enough to think about with Mabel and the accusations about her diamond ring? It might be best to leave the fire and Gwen's death to the experts."

"Well, I have some news about Mabel," I said. "But I'll wait until Gabe is here before I say anything. I don't want to tell the story twice." I was surprised, but when Adam moved closer to me, my first reaction had been to push away from him. It was obvious I wasn't going to be able to trust him until I understood why he'd hidden his relationship with Ron from me. I glanced toward the kitchen. I could hear Gabe getting cups out of the cabinet. "Adam," I said as quietly as I could. "I have to ask you a question."

He smiled at me. "Shoot."

"Why didn't you tell me you know Ron Druther?"

Adam's eyes widened. "How do you know about that?"

"A friend told me. It doesn't matter who it was," I said. "I asked why you didn't tell me."

He was silent and turned his face from me, gazing once again at the crackling flames. Finally he sighed. "Hilde, I'm not a doctor, but I am a professional. I can't divulge details about clients. Yes, Ron is a client, and I knew he'd lost a lot of money in the stock market." He looked at me, his expression solemn. "His fault, by the way; I gave him advice he didn't follow. He needed money and thought he could clean up by making a risky investment. It didn't work out." He ran his hand through his hair. "I wondered about that when I saw the fire. I hope his situation had nothing to do with it."

I wasn't sure how I felt about Adam's response. Was he telling me the truth? Was it a simple case of protecting client confidentiality? Or was there something else at work?

Adam reached for my hand. "Surely you understand. I may mention that someone is a client, but I will never tell you what's going on in their portfolios or divulge personal information. I simply can't do it."

"I—I guess I understand," I said. "It just shocked me to find out you'd withheld something like that from me."

"Something like what?" Gabe stood next to the couch, holding a silver tray with a teapot and cups.

Adam jumped up and took the tray, setting it on the coffee table in front of us. I briefly explained to Gabe that Ron Druther was Adam's client.

"And I would appreciate it if this information wouldn't go any further than this room," Adam said.

"Of course it won't," Gabe said. He picked up the teapot. "This is Wuyi Oolong tea. And to go along with it, I've made some coconut macaroons." He poured the tea, and Adam and I helped ourselves to the macaroons. I bit into the soft, warm cookie. It was yummy and different from any macaroon I'd ever had. The tea had a deep, rich flavor that complemented the dessert perfectly.

"This tea is so good," I said after taking another sip. "I think I've heard of it. Isn't it supposed to help you lose weight?"

Gabe chuckled. "That's what they say. That means you can help yourself to as many cookies as you want, I guess."

Adam laughed. "I feel better about it then. I thought I was too full to eat another bite, but these cookies are great. Did you make them yourself, Gabe?"

He nodded. "They're actually a family recipe, and the tea has been a longtime favorite."

"It's the perfect ending to dinner," I said. "Thank you so much."

"You're welcome." Gabe took a seat in the large wing-back chair to my right. "Now, why don't you catch me up on your day? I assume it was eventful? I wouldn't expect anything less from you."

Adam chortled and spit out a few crumbs. "Sorry," he said, wiping his mouth.

I made a comment about not understanding why he'd found Gabe's remark humorous, but he just shrugged and winked at Gabe.

"If you're both finished poking fun at me, I'd be glad to proceed."

Gabe looked up toward the ceiling. "I think I'm finished for now. How about you, Adam?"

"Well, at least for the next few minutes. Go ahead, Hilde," he said, giving me a smug smile.

"You're both very cute." I took another sip of tea and one more bite of my cookie. Then I started in on my visit to Willowbrook. I tried to downplay my confrontation with Ron. I was a little concerned about an overly macho reaction. Ron had enough problems without either one of them deciding to "defend my honor." When I told them about calling the Winnemakers, Adam stopped me.

"Wait a minute," he said. "What do you mean you remembered the telephone number and address? After only seeing it once?"

I grinned at him. "Do you remember the time Mrs. Kirby, our third-grade teacher, gave you an F for not turning in your geography assignment?"

Adam frowned at me. "Yes, but what does that have to do. . ."

"Remember what had happened to your paper?"

He bit his lip as he tried to bring up the memory. "Oh, yeah. Johnny Frye took my paper and erased my name. He put his on it instead." His eyebrows shot up. "You bailed me out because you'd read my essay. You told Mrs. Kirby exactly what I'd written. I ended up with an A, and Johnny ended up in the principal's office."

I smiled at him. "Didn't you think it was odd that I was able to recall an essay word for word after only seeing it once?"

"You're trying to tell me that you have one of those photographic memories?"

"Good conclusion, Sherlock. It only took you fifteen years to figure it out."

Gabe laughed. "You're going to have to be careful from here on out, Adam. Show her something once—and she'll remember it for life."

Adam look alarmed. "Wow. I'm not sure how I feel about this."

"You just need to use it to your advantage," Gabe said, still grinning. "Let her see a list of your family's birthdays and anniversaries. You'll have her to remind you. You'll never miss another one."

"Hmm. You might be helpful with my Christmas card list, too."

I slapped his arm. "Very funny." I ignored their laughter and finished my story. "So I guess I'm done looking for Mabel. I mean, it's not my problem anymore. To be honest, I've been thinking more about Mabel's dog than I have Mabel since I left the Winnemakers. It's an older dog with asthma. What will happen—" At that moment my phone rang. I'd put my purse on the couch when I came in, so it was easy to reach over and grab it. Unfortunately, it wasn't as easy to find my phone. I fumbled around until my fingers closed around it. I looked at the caller ID. It was Paula. "Do you mind if I take this?" I asked Gabe. "It's Paula. It might be important."

Gabe shook his head. "Please go ahead. I'll warm up the

tea." He got to his feet and picked up the tray.

I answered the phone while Adam stood up and stretched his legs, using the break to stir the embers of the fire.

"Hey, Hilde!" Paula said. "Anything new?"

I quickly told her about my meeting with the Winnemakers and my feeling that I'd done about all I could do to solve the Mabel problem.

"Well, I hate to stir up the pot," Paula said. "But remember that guy I told you I was starting to see? The one who works for the mortuary service?"

I told her I did.

"I was telling him a little bit about your situation. Nothing about the ring or anything that might make you look bad."

"Paula, I really don't want you to tell anyone about this. Even your boyfriend," I said with a sigh.

"I know, I know," she said quickly. "But this is different. Martin actually delivered Mabel to the coroner's office, Hilde. And he brought her back. I didn't tell him anything about your concerns. I just told him you had some questions about her. And I told him Mabel, or whoever she is, was in the fire. That's it. I thought you might want to talk to him. Maybe he can help you find out more about what really happened."

"I—I don't know. Maybe you should just put him in touch with the Winnemakers. It's really in their hands now."

"Hilde," Paula said, "neither one of us can do that. Gus would have a fit if I approached the Winnemakers. And asking Martin to do it won't work either. His boss might fire him. Any impropriety associated with their transportation services—well, it wouldn't be good."

"I—I don't know. . . ."

"Look, why don't you have dinner with Martin and me tomorrow night? Ask your new friend, Adam, to join us." She burst out laughing. "By the way, you really have a warped sense of humor, you know that?"

"What in the world are you talking about? And what's so funny?" I was already a little irritated about being pulled back into the Mabel debacle. Paula's insane cackling wasn't helping my mood.

"Oh, come on, Hilde," she said between gasps. "Surely you've figured it out. You're dating a guy named Adam, and you live in Eden. You're right. There's nothing the least bit funny about that."

"Oh, for goodness' sakes!" I said forcefully. "Adam and Eden. I hadn't thought about it."

A burst of laughter from Adam and Gabe's warm chuckle drifting from the kitchen told me that I was the only one who hadn't seen it.

"Gee, Hilde," Paula said, "for someone so smart, sometimes you're awfully slow."

"Thanks. I appreciate uplifting comments about my intelligence," I said sourly. "If I go tomorrow night, where do you want to meet?"

Paula, finally somewhat subdued, mentioned a popular eastside restaurant. "Be there at seven," she said. Her voice took on a plaintive tone. "Even if you don't care about Martin's possible connection to Mabel, I'd really like you to meet this guy. He could be the one, Hilde."

I couldn't help but sigh. Add Martin to the list of a dozen others who were supposed to be *the one*. "I'll ask Adam and get back to you tomorrow. I'll call you in the afternoon."

I hung up and walked back into the living room. Adam's silly grin made me laugh. "Okay. Adam and Eden. It just didn't occur to me."

Gabe poked his head out from the kitchen. "I may not have a photographic memory, but I caught it the first time you said it."

I felt my face flush. "Man, I can certainly be dense." I looked at Adam, who was sitting on the couch again. "I don't suppose we could call you something else. What's your middle name?"

"Herbert."

I shook my head. "Herbert. No, I don't think so. It's a fine name, but you truly don't look like a Herbert."

"And what does a Herbert look like?" Gabe asked with a grin as he carried in another pot of tea.

"I'm sure I don't know. But Adam isn't one." I reached over to put my cell phone back in my purse and managed to knock it over. The tea bag Mrs. Hudson had given me fell out, and I picked it up. I held it out to Gabe. "Since you're such a tea connoisseur, why don't you take this? Mrs. Hudson is always trying to foist her latest tea creation off on me. You may as well reap the benefits, too."

Gabe took the plastic bag from my hand like he was hold-ing a container of nuclear waste. "Thank you, but she's already dropped off several bags of this offensive stuff. I'm a little afraid my trash hauler won't cart it away without a fee."

Adam looked perplexed. "Aren't you both being a little harsh? I mean, tea is tea, right?"

Gabe shook his head slowly. "Not the way Mrs. Hudson mixes it."

I grinned at him. "Maybe this one will be better. Supposedly Derek, Mrs. Hudson's nephew, bought her some special herbs. My guess is that he was tired of her horrible mixtures and picked up something more appropriate. It might actually be good."

"I doubt that seriously," Gabe said, "but I'll give it a try." He put the plastic bag down on the table and then poured some tea into our empty cups. "If you don't mind, let's go back to your story, Hilde. So you feel that it's time to walk away from Mabel and let her family handle the situation?"

I took a sip from my cup before I answered. "Yes. Now the family knows everything I do. It's up to them."

"And what about the fire and Gwen's death?"

I shrugged. "I have to admit that it bothers me. Maybe it was an accident. Maybe it wasn't. It's the fire department's job to decide if Druther's was destroyed by arson. And I'm sure Ron will be on their radar. There's nothing I can do about it."

Gabe picked up another macaroon and stared at it. "Yes, maybe. . ."

"I think Hilde's right," Adam said. "She's done everything she can. I think she needs to move on."

Gabe stared at him and shook his head. "You might be correct, but there's still something here that doesn't feel right to me."

Adam yawned. "Well, I don't know about you two, but a great dinner and a wonderful dessert have made me sleepy. I'm heading home." He smiled at me. "I'll be by at nine in the morning to pick you up."

"I wish you'd tell me where we're going," I said. "I don't like surprises."

"I guarantee you'll like this one. No one in their right mind could find anything objectionable about this experience."

"Wanna bet?"

He stood up and thanked Gabe for his hospitality. "Maybe you could encourage our gal to get up on the right side of the bed tomorrow—with a good attitude and hope in her heart."

Gabe rose from his chair and patted Adam on the shoulder. "I think I can work on the good attitude, but I'm afraid her heart isn't in my circle of power." He smiled at me. "Let me walk you out," he said to Adam.

"Wait, I'll go with you." I started to pick up my dishes so I could carry them to the kitchen.

"Leave that," Gabe said. "I have a certain way of doing

things. I don't want some woman messing around in my kitchen."

"Oh, so now I'm 'some woman'? Nice." I stepped over and gave Gabe a quick hug. "Well, this woman is going home to get some sleep. It's been a long, long day."

Gabe gently grabbed my arm and whispered in my ear, "I asked your young man to eat with us so I could check him out. I like him. Hang on to him, Hilde."

"I'll try," I whispered back. So that was the reason for the gracious host routine. I liked the fact that Gabe cared about me enough to give my boyfriend the once-over.

As we headed down the stairs, I asked Adam about meeting Paula and her date for dinner.

"Sure, it sounds fine. I'd like to meet some of your friends."

"Paula is a friend, but I don't know this new boyfriend of hers. He works for a mortuary service." Gabe fetched my coat from the bear's arm and held it out while I slipped into it. "She says he actually delivered Mabel to and from the coroner's office. Paula thinks he might know something that could help."

"I thought you were letting this go?" Gabe said.

"I am. But Paula really wants me to meet him anyway. I don't see what it will hurt."

While I buttoned my coat, I sneaked a quick peek behind the counter. The envelope was gone. I walked quickly toward the door, not giving Gabe a chance to see me perusing his personal property.

"Strange turn of events—your friend Paula stumbling across the man who brought the body to the funeral home," Gabe said.

"Not really. Paula works at a funeral home, too. It's a very connected world. She's known this guy for a long time."

"A small but weird world," Adam mumbled.

I smiled at him. "It might seem like a weird world to you, but trust me, what we do is very necessary."

Gabe reached around me and pulled the door open for us. "Yes, otherwise we'd have bodies piling up all over the place. Definitely not an attractive alternative."

I laughed and thanked him once again for the evening. Adam walked me to my car. "I had a wonderful time," he said. "Thanks for not kicking me out. Hope I didn't interfere by popping in."

The wind had picked up strength and pushed black clouds quickly across the sky, allowing only quick glimpses of twinkling stars. They looked like sparkling diamonds in a sea of black velvet. The stars were so much brighter and easier to see in Eden. I pointed them out to Adam. He gazed upward. "Wow. They're beautiful." Then he brought his face close to mine. "And so are you." He kissed me softly on the lips. "You better get home. It's freezing out here."

"I'll see you tomorrow."

He kissed me lightly one more time and turned to go to his car. Before he opened his door, he looked back at me. "Good night, Sleeping Beauty."

When we were kids, I'd told him that my mother woke me up every morning by saying, "Wake up, Sleeping Beauty." I couldn't believe he'd remembered. I'd loved the Disney story about the sleeping princess. And to be honest, standing there in the dark after being kissed by Adam, I felt like a princess.

CHAPTER ELEVEN

The events of the last few days had left me exhausted. When my alarm rang, I almost shut it off and went back to sleep. But the idea of Adam knocking on my door and finding me disheveled, with dried spittle on my face, spurred me into action. I climbed out of bed and grabbed my clothes, my tote full of toiletries, and a towel and washrag and headed for the bathroom. I'd just set everything up in preparation for my shower, when I once again heard voices drifting through the vent. This was getting to be ridiculous. I really didn't want to overhear conversations that weren't my business. At least that's what I told myself as I scooted closer to the opening.

"I don't care," Minnie was saying, "this has got to stop. It's time to call the police."

"I know, I know," Mrs. Hudson responded. "But I've never had anything like this happen before. It's embarrassing. I want to be absolutely certain. . . ."

"Arabella Hudson!" Minnie squeaked. "It has to be Isaiah

Sims. You know I'm not stealing my own things. The only people left are Hilde and. . ."

"Just stop right there," Mrs. Hudson said firmly. "I won't hear a word against Hilde. That girl wouldn't steal. I'm sure of that."

Although it made me feel good to know Mrs. Hudson trusted me, I noticed that she cut Minnie off before she mentioned the only other person in the house. It seemed to me that she wasn't very confident of her nephew's innocence.

I heard some rattling of dishes and a few more muted comments, but I didn't have the time to be any nosier. I was already running behind schedule, so I showered quickly, dressed, and got back to my apartment in record time. I'd just finished brushing my hair and putting on mascara when I heard Adam's car below in the driveway. I grabbed my old coat out of the closet and pulled it on. A once-over in the mirror made me stop cold. In the morning light I realized just how bad the coat really looked. The cracks and tears were past the point of giving it *character*. I looked more like someone who should stand on a street corner with a cardboard sign that reads: WILL WORK FOR FOOD. I didn't know exactly where Adam was taking me, but it was possible some of his friends would be there. Although I didn't want to do it, I took off my coat and got the one my mother gave me out of the closet. To my surprise, it fit perfectly and actually looked good on me. It went great with my slacks and sweater, and it didn't make me look the least bit dorky.

I could hear Adam on the stairs. I quickly grabbed the old leather jacket to hang it up in the closet. When I did, I knocked the book the Winnemakers had given me off the chair and onto the floor. I finished putting my coat away and picked up the book. As I did, an envelope slid out and fell on the floor. I picked it up and put it on top of the book. I wanted to see what it was, but right at that moment, Adam knocked on the door. I ran my hands through my hair once more and plastered a smile on my face.

"Wow!" he said when I swung the door open. "I see how you stay so thin. Three flights of stairs day after day would keep anyone in shape."

I ushered him into my room, but I kept the door open. Mrs. Hudson's rule. Of course, I'd never had to worry about that particular edict before. I made a sweeping motion with my hand and added a little bow. "This is it. My palace."

Adam stood in the middle of the room and looked around. "I really like it, Hilde," he said with a grin. "It's so cozy and. . .well. . .you."

I wasn't sure what he meant by that, but I was pretty sure it was a compliment. "Thanks. I love it." I went over to the windows and opened the shades. "I have a pretty neat view, too."

He came up next to me and gazed through the windows. "Yes, you do. The only thing I can see from my windows are the neighbors across the street. You've got me beat by a mile."

Standing so close to him made me feel funny and great

all at the same time. I enjoyed it a few more moments, then I took his arm and led him over to my dresser.

"And this is Sherlock, my friend and companion." The little goldfish swam up next to the side of his bowl and looked Adam over.

Adam laughed. "Why, I could swear he just waved at me."

When he said that, I realized I really was falling in love with Adam Sawyer. I mean, a man who can actually see my goldfish wave is a man I can get serious with.

"See you, Sherlock." Adam waved back at my little gold friend and grinned at me. "Are you ready?"

"Yes, but I wish you'd give me some idea where we're going. I have no idea if I'm dressed right."

He looked me up and down. "You're dressed perfectly." He ran his fingers down the sleeve of my coat. "I love this coat. It looks great on you."

I wanted to argue with him—tell him that it couldn't look that good since my mother picked it out, but I knew he was right. "Thanks," I said grudgingly. "We'd better get going before Mrs. Hudson comes up here to see if anything untoward is going on."

"Untoward, huh? I'm not sure what all that entails, but we may have to look into it one of these days."

"As far as Mrs. Hudson is concerned, the fact that you're even here is pushing the envelope quite a bit. We'd better skedaddle before my reputation is completely shattered."

Adam gently guided me to the door. "We certainly can't

have that. Let's get out of here while your character is still unsullied."

"Thank you. I appreciate your chivalry, kind sir."

Adam bowed with a flourish and a grin. "No problem. Besides, I'd like to come back sometime. I can't take any chances on alienating Mrs. Hudson. So far, she seems to like me."

He was right. When we came down the stairs, Mrs. Hudson was standing near the front door, a big smile on her face. "I wondered if you two young people might like a cup of hot tea before you go out into the cold."

The smell of stinky tea emanated from the kitchen. The current mixture smelled even worse than some of her earlier versions. There was an odd aroma—something I didn't recognize—kind of like wet hay. It was enough to make Adam smile and push me hurriedly toward the door.

"I'm dreadfully sorry, Mrs. Hudson, but we're running a little late. Maybe some other time?"

Although she looked disappointed, her wide smile told me she was properly impressed by Adam. Mrs. Hudson has her faults, but she has always been kind to me. Sometimes I wonder if she sees me as the daughter she never had. Mrs. Hudson's husband died when he was young. She never married again and never had any children. As far as I know, Derek is her only living relative.

"Anytime, Mr. Sawyer. Maybe you could come to our next residents' dinner?" Her question was directed to him, but she was looking at me.

"Thank you, Mrs. Hudson. That would be lovely," I said with a smile. She frowned on asking those outside our house to our special dinners. This was quite a privilege.

Adam flashed her one of his most charming smiles and ushered me out the door. When it closed behind us, he put his arm around me and escorted me down the stairs. "What in the world was that smell?" he whispered in my ear. "Was it really tea?"

"See what I mean? I think it's getting worse. I couldn't even begin to identify this one. Sometimes I can figure out what's in it—except for the stinky feet one. I have no idea what that is."

Adam held the car door open for me. "Perhaps it really is stinky feet," he said. "If you come up missing any socks. . ."

I waited until he opened his car door and got inside. "My feet don't stink," I said sharply.

"Oh. Pardon me. I've found a girl with feet that smell like roses. I'm very impressed."

With that, he leaned over and kissed me. I reached up and put my hand on the side of his face. When he pulled away, I smiled sweetly at him. "And don't you forget it, bub."

"I am properly chastised. Now put your seat belt on. I don't want to take any chances with you. Mrs. Hudson would never forgive me if I returned you even slightly damaged."

Neither Adam nor I brought up the subject of Mabel. I think we both needed a break. He talked about the office where he worked and how obsessed some of the other brokers were with their jobs. "I don't ever want my career to take over my life," he said. "My dad worked hard to support us, but I would have traded time with him for almost any of the *things* he provided for us. Our pastor talks a lot about setting priorities. God first, family second, ministry third, and job fourth. I'm trying to get my ducks in a row now so I won't have a problem when I get married someday." He looked over at me and smiled. "I guess what you'll see today is the *ministry* part of my life."

I looked out the car window. We were driving past a local hospital. Adam turned in and headed for the parking lot.

"We're going to the hospital? I hope you're not an undercover doctor. One in the family is enough."

"No, I'm not a doctor. Not even a candy striper, although I think I'd look adorable in the outfit."

"I'm sure you would," I said laughing. "Hopefully, I can get that image out of my mind now."

Adam parked the car, and we got out. He opened the trunk of his car and removed a large suitcase with wheels. He set it down on the ground and pulled out the handle so he could roll it. Then he shut the trunk.

"So you need a suitcase to do this thing?" I said. "Hmm. There's not a body in there, is there?"

Adam smiled. "No. No body."

He turned to walk toward the entrance, and I followed him. We went through the lobby, straight over to the elevators. Another man came running toward us as the doors opened.

"Adam! Hold the elevator!" he called out.

Adam put his hand against the doors before they could close. "Hi, Harold. You almost didn't make it."

Harold was large, with a rather florid face. His hairline was definitely receding, and he had combed most of his remaining strands forward in an attempt to fool people, I guess. It wasn't working, obviously, since I'd spotted his deception so easily.

"Harold, this is my friend Hilde," Adam said as the elevator doors closed. "She doesn't know what we do, so don't say anything. I want to surprise her."

Harold's laugh was from his gut. "Nice to meet you, Hilde," he said. "I hope seeing Adam for who he really is won't chase you away. He's taking a big chance."

I reached out and took the hand he'd extended toward me. "Unless you guys are planning to rob sick people, I don't think there's anything that could upset me enough to dump him. Unfortunately, I think I'm starting to get used to him."

Harold guffawed again. "I understand. He's kind of like fungus. He keeps growing on you."

I smiled at him, but before I could say anything else, the doors opened. We stepped out into the children's wing of the hospital. My stomach knotted. A rather long spell spent in the hospital when I was a kid made me a little overly sensitive to this place. I didn't remember much about it, but being here brought back an odd feeling of déjà vu. The surroundings didn't look familiar, but the antiseptic smell jogged something down deep inside of me. I felt a little woozy for a moment but reminded myself I was now an adult and that those days were behind me.

"Are you okay?" Adam asked. He tightened his grip on my arm and looked at me with a worried expression.

"I'm fine," I said. "Sorry. I got dizzy for a second, but it's passed. Where do we go from here?"

His hand slipped down and took mine. "This way."

We followed Harold down a long hallway, stopping at the door to a large room. "Take a seat in here, Hilde," Adam whispered. "We'll be back in a few minutes."

I nodded and let go of his hand. The room was full of children and nurses. There were also quite a few adults sitting in chairs at the back. Most of the children sat on the floor. The nurses were scattered throughout the room. Everyone was focused on the front of the room where a young woman sat perched on a stool, holding a puppet in her hands. I sat down quietly, next to a young couple who held each other's hands. I wondered if one of the children belonged to them. I couldn't imagine what it would be like to have a child who was seriously ill. Even though I couldn't recall many details of my hospital experience, probably because I didn't want to, I could still remember the look on my mother's and father's faces. The fear in their eyes. Funny how I hadn't thought about it for so long. The memory brought back emotions I'd tried to forget. The fear, the longing to go home, and most of all, the way I'd depended on my parents to make everything okay. I felt my eyes fill with tears as I gazed around the room at the families who were experiencing what would most probably be remembered as one of the worst times in their lives. I doubted that the joy of recovery wiped away the days and nights of worry and despair. I know Mom's faith got her through our episode. God is good, and He answered our prayers. But for years after I recovered, anytime I felt sick, I could see that familiar spark of panic in my mother's eyes.

I forced myself to quit thinking about the past and concentrated on the young woman trying so hard to entertain the boys and girls who watched her with eager faces. Their laughter confirmed that she was hitting her mark. Her puppet was an odd-looking rabbit with big ears and a goofy expression. Her repartee was quick and humorous. I began to forget about the drama around me and actually enjoyed the show. When she stopped, the kids hollered with glee, and the young woman blushed at their enthusiastic response. I was thinking about how her efforts were actually a wonderful ministry when a man in a suit stepped up to the front of the room.

"Thank you, Sandy and Floppy, for that great show. Now, boys and girls, it's my pleasure to welcome back a group that's a favorite here. Say hello to Binky, BamBam, BoBo, Buttons, and Buttercup—Clowns for Christ!"

Five men dressed in clown suits ran into the room. As the children yelled out with delight, one of them winked at me.

It was the last thing I saw before I passed out.

CHAPTER TWELVE

"Hilde. Hilde, open your eyes. You're fine. Open your eyes."

I forced my eyelids apart and found my mother bending over me. What was she doing here? Better yet, what was I doing here? And where was *here*? "Where am I?" I asked. I would have liked to have said something less cliché, but there it was.

"You're in the hospital. You passed out and bumped your head. You'll be fine, but you'll probably have a pretty good headache."

"But how did you. . . I mean, why are you. . ."

My mother looked at me the way she does when I do or say something especially dumb. "I work here, Hilde. You do remember that, right?"

I struggled to sit up. I was lying on a gurney in an examination room. My mother was right. Pain shot through my head like fire. "Ouch! Of course I know you work here, Mother," I said as softly as I could so as not to offend my damaged skull any further. "But why are you here now?"

Mom crossed her arms and frowned at me. Standing there in her white coat with her name tag on display, I felt more like a bad patient than a bad daughter.

"Judy was in the room. She recognized you and called me after you hit the floor."

Judy Roberts has been my mother's nurse assistant for many years. She is a lovely lady with a sweet voice and the ability to put patients at ease. She balances out my mother's no-nonsense personality perfectly.

"Where's. . .where's. . ."

"Where's your boyfriend the clown?" My mother arched one eyebrow and stared at me. Although her expression was quite serious, I could have sworn the corners of her mouth twitched a little.

"Oh my," I moaned. I fell back on the fluffy pillow that had been placed under my head. "He must think I'm mental."

"I take it you had no idea Adam's stage name is *Buttercup*."

I moaned again. "Buttercup? It just gets better and better."

This time I was certain my mother covered her mouth to hide a smile. Yeah, this was funny all right. I was falling in love with a man who liked to put on makeup, call himself by the name of a delicate flower, and scare people like me half to death.

Mom pulled a pad out of her coat pocket and scribbled something on it. "Here's a prescription for something a little stronger than over-the-counter pain reliever. I'm only giving you a few. Your headache should disappear in a day or two."

I took the note she held out. "Thanks, Mom. I won't use this unless I have to."

My mother shook her head. My aversion to medicine was another one of my quirks, but the sharp pain in my head almost convinced me that this one time I might be willing to cross the line and pop a few pills.

"Whatever, Hilde. But I insist that you call me later today and let me know how you're doing."

I nodded my agreement, but slowly, trying to avoid severe distress.

"I'm going to let Adam in to see you. He's been very concerned." She patted me on the shoulder. It was a small show of compassion, but for my mother, it was quite demonstrative. "I explained to him about your 'clown thing.' I think he understands."

Ignoring the ache in my head, I sat up again. "My *clown thing*? You told him I have a ridiculous fear of clowns and I have no idea why? That's great, Mother. Now he's going to really think I'm wacko."

Mom looked down at the floor silently for several seconds. Finally, she looked up at me. I was surprised to see tears in her eyes. "Hilde, I can't believe you don't really know why you hate clowns. This experience today should have brought it all back clearly."

And then I realized it had. I'd pushed the memory so far

back in my mind, even seeing Adam and his friends hadn't jiggled it loose. But seeing my mother cry did. "There were clowns in the hospital, weren't there? When I was sick."

Mother nodded. She couldn't have looked more uncomfortable if she had accidentally swallowed her stethoscope. "Somehow you transferred the fear of your time here to them."

"If you knew this, why didn't you tell me?" I asked. "You knew I hated clowns."

"For goodness' sakes, Hilde," she said sharply. "The last time you mentioned it was years ago. I'd hoped you'd grown out of it."

"The last time I mentioned it? What about the time our third-grade class went to the circus, and the teacher had to carry me out of the place screaming? You didn't think that was a good time to bring it up?"

She shook her head and rubbed the back of her neck. "I didn't want to talk about it. Your illness was a horrible time in our lives. I didn't want to remind you of it, and I certainly didn't want to relive it. I thought you'd get over it. I mean, the clowns had nothing to do with the reason you were in the hospital. Besides, you were so young. . . ."

"Well, I didn't *get over it*. I really wish you'd—"

"I've got patients waiting." Her words were short and quick, like little machine gun bursts. "I'll send Adam in. Call me later."

With that and a swish of her lab coat, she was gone, leaving me more than a little annoyed. At least now I remembered why I hated clowns. The question remained, though, how would this affect my relationship with Adam?

The door to the exam room swung open slowly, and he slowly walked into the room. He'd removed his little hat with the flower, along with his red wig. He'd also tried to wipe off his makeup, but there were still strange little streaks near his ears and mouth. And he sported the remnants of a second set of eyebrows that arched high above his own natural ones. He wore an oversize red jacket over a bright yellow shirt and polka-dot tie. His black-and-white-striped pants were too short and brought attention to his extremely large shoes. The toes flapped as he walked across the room. He stopped a few feet from the gurney.

"Hi," he said gently, as if I were a mental patient he didn't want to send into a frenzy. Although I didn't want to be treated with kid gloves, I had to admit that his costume made my stomach feel queasy and the hairs on the back of my neck stand up.

"Hi. Sorry I caused such a big scene out there. I hope I didn't ruin your show."

He smiled and came closer. "No. Binky—I mean, Harold—made a joke out of it. He told the kids that every time I come into a room, women faint. They thought it was funny."

"Oh, great. Glad I could provide some comic relief. Maybe I should join your group. Everyone's name starts with a *B*, huh? Maybe I could be 'Brain Damaged.'"

A burst of laughter escaped Adam's lips before he noticed my expression. He cut it short. "Look, Hilde," he said, "your mother told me about your illness when you were a child and that you're afraid of clowns because of it. I'm really sorry. If I'd known. . ."

I pushed the hair out of my eyes and smiled at him. "It happened before you moved to the neighborhood. My mother and I don't talk about it. There's no way you could have known. Besides, what would you have done? Quit your clown gig to make me happy?"

Adam frowned but didn't say anything.

"Don't worry. I would never ask you to do that. I realize what a great thing you're doing for these children. I'll just have to get used to it. And I will."

Adam sighed with relief and grabbed my hand. "Are you sure you can? We'll take it slow, Hilde. You don't have to come when we perform—until you're ready." He kissed my fingers. "Frankly, if you never see our show, that's okay. I can keep this part of my life to myself."

I squeezed his hand. "That won't work. If we're going to continue seeing each other, I'm going to have to get over this. You can help me." I grinned at him. "Kind of like shock therapy."

His eyes narrowed. "Sure. Whatever you need, but do you think you'll keep passing out during our performances? It's a little disturbing."

I laughed, sending waves of pain through my head. "I promise. No more fainting. Now, help me off this thing. I want to go home, if you're finished." As he helped me climb down from the gurney, I asked him, "What about your performance? Is it still going on?"

"Don't worry about it. The other guys can carry the show."

I slid down from the cart and into his arms. I tried hard not to look at his outfit, but it was difficult. Not too many clothing combinations use almost every color imaginable. "Again, I'm sorry, Adam. I really am."

He hugged me close, and his plastic flower jabbed into my cheek. "It's okay. I'm almost glad it happened. I re-acquainted myself with your lovely mother, and now I know more about you. Except for the bump on your head, it was almost worth it."

Little did he know that his "lovely mother" comment didn't endear him to me. "Okay," I said, pulling back. "Could you take me home? And maybe we could stop and get this prescription filled on the way? I told Paula we might meet her tonight, but I need to lie down for a while and see if I can lick this whopper of a headache."

"Sure. We'll stop by the pharmacy. And if you still want to go tonight, I'll pick you up. I don't think you should be driving."

I had no intention of arguing with him. I planned to take my pills and be a good little girl. My head felt like it was being squeezed in a vise.

When we got in the car, Adam pressed a button that lowered the back of my seat. I lay back and closed my eyes, trying to ignore the pain. True to his word, he stopped to get the prescription filled. I started to doze off, but he woke me up to ask me for my driver's license so the pharmacy would release the medication to him. I'd started to fall asleep again when he got back to the car. I opened one eye and looked at him. He was holding a small cup of water.

"Here," he said, handing it to me along with one of the pills. "I thought you might like to take one now. We're still a ways from Eden."

"Oh, thank you. I usually try to avoid medicine, but I don't seem to have a lot of choice in the matter."

"You know, my mother always prayed for me before she gave me any medication. She believes it's important that we never put ourselves at the mercy of men's solutions to God's answers."

I smiled at him even though it hurt. "I love that, Adam. Would you like to pray for me?"

He nodded, closed his eyes, and put his hand on my shoulder. "God, we thank You for being the true Healer. Thank You for touching Hilde with Your power. We know that nothing is stronger than You and that no pain can stand in Your presence. We also pray this medicine will be a blessing to her body. Thank You."

When I opened my eyes, I already felt more relaxed. I took the pill, but I knew it was my secondary answer. Not my first. I took a few more sips of water and put the cup in his cup holder.

"Thanks again," I said. "And thanks for going in to get the medicine." I looked at his costume. "You could have changed clothes at the hospital, you know. I'm sure you got some strange looks."

He shrugged. "I didn't want you to have to wait for me."

"At least you took off your big shoes. I'm grateful. Getting in an accident on top of everything else would have been awful." I noticed a couple of the store's employees looking out the window at our car. I pointed them out to Adam. "You must have made quite an impression."

He grinned. "Well, they certainly looked over your driver's license more than once. And I think the pharmacist sent one of his assistants to make sure you were really in the car."

I couldn't help but giggle at the image in my mind. But laughter wasn't my friend yet. At least the sharp ache had dulled somewhat. "Ouch. I think I need to get home."

Adam put the car in gear and drove out of the parking lot. Although we'd been quiet after leaving the hospital, this time the silence was different. I looked over at him and caught him glancing my way.

"Is there something you wanted to say?" I asked.

"No. Yes. Well, no. I was just curious about something, but if you don't want to tell me, you don't have to."

"I can't think of anything you can't ask me, Adam. What is it?"

"Your stay in the hospital when you were a kid. What was it for?"

It was silly, but I didn't want to tell him. My mother and I never spoke about it. But I couldn't just sit there like a statue.

"It. . .it was. . .leukemia."

Adam didn't speak for a moment. Then all he said was, "Wow."

I turned my sore head toward the window. The memories of needles and tubes fought to get inside my head. Blood counts and pain. Fear. "I don't like to think about it."

"I'm sorry, Hilde. I didn't know." He reached over and put his hand on my arm. "I'm sure it was a scary experience. I'm so grateful you recovered."

I turned back toward him. "Me, too. God was certainly with me. I may have blocked a lot of the experience from my mind, but I've never forgotten how close I felt to Him during that time. If I didn't love Him for anything else, I would love Him for that alone. Someday I'll tell you about it. But not today."

He lightly rubbed my arm. "You know," he said softly, "He will help you get rid of the fear, too. If you give it to Him."

"I know that, Adam. I don't know why it's been so hard. I really don't want to be afraid. But sometimes I worry the leukemia will come back."

"But God doesn't want you to live in fear. He wants you to live in faith."

I nodded. "I've told Paula that worry is an insult to God. I really believe that, but this thing still lingers inside for some reason."

Adam laughed. "I think God is trying to tell you that the time has come. I mean, sending a clown into your life must mean something."

"Yes," I said wryly. "It means He has a twisted sense of humor."

Adam chuckled. "You know what, you're right. Sometimes He does. I kind of love that about Him."

"Yeah, me, too. It makes me feel like He really understands me." Even though I'd only taken the pill a few minutes earlier, I began to feel abnormally sleepy. The last word in my sentence had trailed off, making it sound like I said God "understands mehhhh." I didn't want to fall asleep in Adam's car, but before I could help myself, my eyes closed. The next thing I remembered was Adam holding me up as we climbed the stairs to my apartment. I didn't see Mrs. Hudson anywhere around, but Derek appeared and held my door open while Adam got me inside. About two hours later, I woke up on top of my bed, my shoes off and my grandmother's quilt tucked around me. I sat up slowly. The pain had turned into a dull throbbing. I swung my legs over the side of the bed and tried to get to my feet. Still a little woozy, it was difficult to stand up without swaying a little.

I noticed a piece of paper propped up in my chair, so I practiced regaining my sea legs by navigating a course toward it. I finally made it, grabbed the note, and sat down in the chair. It was from Adam.

> *Dear Hilde,*
>   *Hope you feel better when you wake up. I will call you around five. If you still feel like meeting your friend Paula, I will pick you up around six thirty.*
>   *Adam*

> *P.S. You really are a sleeping beauty.*

Oh, brother. My mother has told me for years that I "snore like a sailor," whatever that means. I have no idea how sailors sound when they snore, so I had nothing to compare it to.

I got up again and headed for the bathroom. I couldn't see the bump on the back of my head, but I could sure feel it. A look in the mirror revealed a pale face and unfocused pupils. Great. I looked like some kind of drug addict. No more pain pills for me.

I washed my face with cold water, and it helped to wake me up a little. Then I made a Monte Cristo sandwich with SPAM® Oven Roasted Turkey. It was crispy and delicious. The Muenster cheese accompanied the meat perfectly. I felt a little better after I finished eating. As I heated up some water for tea, my phone rang. It was Rachel at Slumberland. A job for Monday morning. I agreed on a time and hung up. Then I checked my messages. Four new appointments. I would have felt better if Ron had clearly told me he wasn't going to pursue his charges, but maybe life was going to go on after all. Maybe life was going to go on after all. Mabel's family had what they needed, and I hadn't lost my source of income. Of course, if Alfred and Edith went after Druther's for misplacing their aunt, it was possible things could get stirred up again. However, after confronting my clown fears, somehow Ron Druther didn't seem quite so scary.

I fixed a cup of tea and carried it to the window seat. A few sips, and I began to feel even better. Raspberry tea is one of my favorite things, but I have to sneak boxes of it into my apartment so Mrs. Hudson won't know I'm not drinking her horrible potions.

The day was gray and cloudy, and the ground was still covered in white. I love days like this. They make me feel cozy and comfortable. Even though the remnants of my frightening clown confrontation tickled the corners of my mind, I felt peaceful inside. My feelings for Adam were stronger than my fear of clowns—and finally facing the reason I'd been lugging around this unreasonable phobia seemed to drain its power over me.

I glanced at the clock. It was almost three. I still had three and a half hours before Adam picked me up. I toyed with the idea of canceling tonight's dinner. I really wasn't interested in what Paula's new boyfriend had to say about Mabel, but I knew she wanted me to meet him. Besides, if he did have any new revelations, and if they would help the Winnemakers put Mabel to rest, I was certainly willing to pass the information along. I liked the odd little couple and wanted to help them if I could.

Thinking about them reminded me about the envelope that had fallen out of the book they'd given me. I was a little surprised to have forgotten it, but clowns and head bumps can push things right out of a person's mind.

I got up and took the envelope from the table. Then I sat down in my comfy chair and looked at it. In shaky handwriting, the name *William* was scrawled on the front. William? Mabel's grandson? I thought about leaving it unopened and returning it to the Winnemakers, but I didn't want to bother them if it wasn't anything important. The envelope wasn't sealed. I pulled out a folded piece of paper. It was a letter from Mabel to William.

Dearest William,

I miss you so very much. Your Love and concern for me seems almost Mysterious. I don't know what I have done to Deserve you. I want you to know how much I appreciate the way you've handled my Affairs. Everything here is Fine. Alfred and Edith are treating me very well—with great Style. Especially Alfred.

I hope to see you Very soon. It is Important to Me That I Convey to You how much I love you. I

Hope you get the chance to Come to Wichita before
long. You will Always have a Home with me.
I will ask Alfred to send this letter out today.
He handles all my mail.

Your loving grandmother

The letters were large and written with very dark ink. Some of the words ran together, while others were capitalized when they shouldn't have been. My grandmother's writing had looked the same after her eyesight began to fail. The date at the top of the page indicated that it was written just a few days before I ran into Mabel at Druther's. Obviously, she had never gotten the chance to ask Alfred to mail it. I folded the letter and put it back in the envelope. I would return it to the Winnemakers so they could give it to William. I was pretty sure it would mean a great deal to all of them. At least it seemed that in life, Mabel was a happy woman. I was glad to find that out. It made me feel better for her, but I still had that silly dog on my mind. I thought about calling the humane society to see how he was faring, but I was a little afraid to hear bad news.

I put the letter on top of my dresser and called Adam. My head only hurt a little now, so I decided to go ahead with dinner. Adam seemed glad to hear from me and confirmed that he would pick me up at six thirty.

After that, I called my mother. Amazingly, she actually answered the phone. I was used to leaving voice messages and waiting for her return calls. I told her I was feeling better.

"Did you take those pills, Hilde?"

"Yes, Mother. And I almost passed out. I feel like a worn-out dishrag."

"But your head feels better?" she asked, sounding rather triumphant.

I sighed. "Yes. Yes, I feel better. They helped. Thank you."

Sometimes giving my mother what she wants seems to confuse her. There were a few moments of silence on the line while I waited for her to recover from my compliment. Finally, she said, "Well, okay. Good. Now, are you still coming over tomorrow?"

"Yes. I'll be there right after church. What are we having?"

"I. . .I thought I'd make some chili."

"I'm sorry, Mother. It must be this head injury. I thought you said you were making chili." I laughed at the ridiculousness of my statement. My mother didn't cook. Not anymore. Ever since she'd become successful, she *picked up* food. I'd concluded that this was the rich socialite's substitution for actually preparing something. "Picking it up" implied some kind of effort that should, in effect, afford the "picker upper" credit for the meal's creation. My mother's usual pickups came from a local restaurant-slash-deli-slash-grocery store that offered gourmet meals already prepared. All the purchaser had to do was heat and eat.

"I did say I was making chili, Hilde," Mom said stiffly. "If I remember right, it was one of your very favorite meals when you were young. I still have the recipe, and I intend to cook it today so we can heat it up after church tomorrow."

I was so flabbergasted I couldn't speak for several seconds. "Was I more severely injured than you let on, Mother? Is there something you're not telling me?"

"Oh, for goodness' sakes, Hildegard. You're so exasperating. I simply want to do something nice for you. I thought you would like some homemade chili, but if it's too much for you to bear. . ."

"No. Please, Mother. I would love to have some of your chili. I'll be there as soon as I get out of church."

"That will be fine. Thank you for calling me to give me an update on your condition."

It was only the clicking and the buzz in my ear that informed me our strange conversation was over. I clicked off my phone then stared at it for a while, as if it could somehow explain what had just happened. Unfortunately, I didn't receive any revelation. I put the phone down and looked toward Sherlock, who was watching me with interest.

"I have no idea," I said to my curious fish. "One of us might be dying from a terminal disease. Either that, or my mother is trying to mend fences. Do you think that's possible?"

Sherlock didn't say anything, but I'm pretty sure he nodded. We'd had lots of conversations—mostly one-sided—but I'd gotten pretty good at interpreting his subtle language clues. I'm fairly certain he was as amazed as I was.

I quickly called Paula to let her know Adam and I would meet her for dinner. Then I got cleaned up and dressed. By the time I was ready to go, it was still only five twenty. I called Adam and asked him to pick me up at Gabe's. I really wished the old man would get a phone. I didn't like just dropping in.

I fed Sherlock, put on my new coat, and headed downstairs. There wasn't anyone around. I assumed Mrs. Hudson was out with Minnie, and Isaiah was wherever he went every day. Derek may have been home, but I couldn't tell. I was happy not to run into him. I decided to leave the car parked. I trudged across the snow-covered road, frozen crystals crunching under my boots. I couldn't help but compare the quiet of Eden with the noise and distraction of Wichita. I enjoy being near a large city, but I have no desire to live there. Give me the silence of the country where you can actually hear birds calling to one another and where you can see too many stars to count in the night skies.

It only took me a couple of minutes to get to Gabe's front door. I knocked first and then pushed it open. The store was deserted. I called out his name but didn't hear a response. Feeling like an intruder, I slowly climbed the stairs.

"Gabe? Are you here?" Like he could possibly be anywhere else. Once again, Mrs. Hudson's concern that one day we'd find Gabe Bashevis dead in his strange antiques store rumbled around inside me. I was really going to have to quit allowing my landlady's fears to wiggle their way into my mind.

As I entered the living room, I spotted him on the couch, stretched out with the newspaper lying across his chest. Next to him sat a glass of water and his bottle of pills. I could see his chest rising and falling, so I knew he was only asleep. I crept quietly up to the table where the pills were and slowly picked up the bottle. Nitroglycerin. I wasn't surprised. Gabe had heart problems. I carefully put the bottle back on the table.

"You're getting a little nosy, aren't you?"

The sound of his voice startled me, and that strange noise I make when I'm frightened pushed past my lips before I could stop it. Gabe's glare turned into a look of amazement—and then he laughed.

"What in heaven's name was that?" he asked, his eyes wide. "Sounded kind of like a cross between a stuck pig and a squeaky grocery cart."

I sat down in the chair across from him. "And just how would you know what a stuck pig sounds like?" I asked innocently. "And since you never go out, how would you ever hear a squeaky grocery cart?"

He pulled himself upright and looked at me with amusement. "How do you imagine my shelves and refrigerator get filled? Do you think elves come at night? Of course I go out. And quit changing the subject. Why are you snooping around my medicine? Do you imagine that it's any of your business?"

I sighed. "I'm just preparing for the day I come in here

and find you dead. I need to tell the paramedics about your medical condition."

Gabe's arched brows framed the twinkle in his eyes. "I'm happy to see you're preparing for my demise. I feel the need to inform you, however, that I don't intend to kick the bucket for a while. So you can relax and quit your rather ghoulish plans."

"Okay. I'll try to think of something different. But it won't be easy."

He shook his head. "You're something else, Hilde Higgins. You know that? Something else."

"I'm not sure what that means, but I'll take it as a compliment."

"That's your choice," he said with a smile. Then he folded up the newspaper and put it on the table. "While we're at it, I want to tell you something. I only intend to say this once, and I expect you to pay attention." His face lost its jovial expression. "I understand that you have a photographic memory. I also understand that you care about your friends. I suspect you not only remember the address and names printed on the package you delivered to me several days ago, but that you may have had a look at the material inside."

I started to protest, to explain that I hadn't purposely invaded his privacy, but he held up his hand for me to be quiet.

"You don't need to explain. I'm pretty sure I know how it happened. The point is—it happened." He folded his arms over his chest and leaned back against the couch. His eyes bored into mine. "If we are to be friends, I must ask you to never bring up that envelope or anything about it. There are some things about my life which must remain completely private. If you cannot respect this boundary, I'm afraid we can't be friends. I do not intend to break down in a moment of emotion and change my mind about this. I will never, ever explain anything about that package or its contents. And I will never give you any details of my past life. That is the way it is, and that is the way it will stay. Do you understand what I'm saying to you, and can you agree to these terms?"

I nodded, but I didn't really understand. Was Gabriel Bashevis an escaped convict? In the Witness Protection Program? An undercover spy? Basically he was telling me that I would never find out the truth. My natural nosiness fought a brief battle with my feelings for the elderly man.

"All right. I truly believe you can trust me with anything, Gabe, but if that's what you want, I'll abide by it."

He nodded. "Believe me, Hilde. It's not what I want, but it's what must be." He picked up his bottle of nitroglycerin. "However, my secrets don't include my medical condition. I do have a slight heart problem. It is controlled by these little white pills. So you don't need to worry. Nor do you and the indomitable Mrs. Hudson need to keep up a death vigil for me. When my graduation day arrives, it will happen somewhere far away from here. I have no intention of allowing my friends to carry that burden."

"Well, I think *real* friends are there for you no matter what," I said. "But I'll try to respect your wishes. I do have to point out, however, that you used the F-word in its plural sense. Does this mean that you now count Mrs. Hudson among your friends?"

Gabe shivered noticeably. "I make no such claim, and if you ever repeat that to anyone else, I will insist that you are mentally deficient and in need of immediate hospitalization."

I couldn't help but smile at his pronouncement, but I was more than a little bothered by his request to keep so much of his life secreted in the shadows. My curiosity was almost stretched to the breaking point.

"Now," he said, rising to his feet, "let's move on to something else. I have an important question for you. Would you come with me into the kitchen, please?"

I obediently rose to my feet and followed him. He pointed at a chair, and I sat down. He remained standing, leaning against the kitchen counter.

"Before I ask you this question, which has been burning in my mind, is there any specific reason you've come to visit today—besides to stick your nose in my personal medical history?"

I made a face at him. "No. I'm just killing time until Adam picks me up for dinner. I couldn't think of anything more enjoyable than spending time with a crotchety old codger like you. It's a sad testament to my life, don't you think?"

"You're very, very funny. I think the last person I saw

with a sense of humor like yours was on *The Gong Show.* Fortunately, he was pulled off the stage."

I scratched my head and stared at him. "What's *The Gong Show?* It must have been before my time. I take it that you watched it in black and white? You might be surprised to learn that there are shows in color now. It's a whole new revolution."

"I have a television, smarty-pants. It's hidden away. I only take it out when I think there is something worth watching. It hasn't seen the light of day in many months now."

"Kind of like you?" I asked dryly.

"Let's get back to talking about you, young lady." He grabbed something from the cabinet and tossed it on the table. Then he sat down across from me. "I know you're wondering if I'm some criminal on the lam. I'm not. I'm afraid you're closer to being incarcerated than I am."

I picked up the plastic bag of Mrs. Hudson's stinky tea I'd left with him the night before. "What are you talking about?"

He grinned. "If you were a child of the sixties, you'd know exactly what I meant."

"My mother was barely a child of the sixties."

Gabe waved his arm with a flourish. "Your stinky tea is a mixture of tea and pot, my dear."

"Pot?" I said, not quite understanding what he meant.

"Pot. Weed. Grass. Reefer. Ganja. Or in more precise terms, marijuana."

I could feel my mouth drop open, but I couldn't seem to control it. "Marijuana? Marijuana! Are you serious? What. . . I mean, how. . . I mean, where. . ."

"Before you get to *who*, let me answer it for you. Didn't you say Mrs. Hudson's nephew gave her some special herbs?"

I nodded slowly. My brain felt fuzzy, and not just from my bump on the head. "She said Derek hid it from her so he could surprise her, but she found it when she was changing his bedsheets." I stared at Gabe, my mind finally processing his shocking revelation. "Oh my goodness. He wasn't trying to keep it under wraps because it was a surprise—he was just stashing it." I thought for a moment. "The thefts around the apartment—I bet they're tied into this somehow." I picked up the plastic bag and gazed at it. "What should I do?"

"I think you ought to tell Mrs. Hudson the truth," he said. "It's her house and her nephew. Let her deal with it."

"This will break her heart. She loves Derek."

He shrugged. "If she really does, she'll make him responsible for his actions. It's the only thing that will help him."

"Well, until I tell her about this, what. . .what about. . ."

"What about the pot?" Gabe smiled. "I'll keep it for you. I don't think it would be a good idea for you to be found with it in your purse. Especially with that theft charge hanging over your head. It just looks bad."

"You're a real comedian. You know I didn't take that ring."

He shook his head sadly. "That's what all career criminals say."

I was trying to come up with something equally caustic when Gabe's front door alarm went off. He stood up and headed into the living room.

I trailed behind him. "Why didn't your little intruder alert work when I came in?"

"I'm afraid I may need to turn up the volume. Seems I slept through it."

"Must be old age," I murmured. "I understand the hearing is the first to go."

"Strange," he said. "I heard it was your taste in friends." He flipped the cover open on his desk and turned on his surveillance screen. Adam waved at the camera. "It's your boyfriend. Why don't you run down and let him in?"

I glanced at my watch. "We probably need to get going. I'll just leave with him." I put my coat on and walked over to where Gabe stood. "Are you ever going to get a phone?"

"I doubt it. Besides, if I had a phone, you might never come to visit."

I leaned over and kissed him on the cheek. "You're wrong about that, old man. I'd come anyway." I smiled at him. "You keep that pot hidden, you hear me? I don't have the money to bail you out of jail."

"If I get caught, I intend to tell the police you gave it to me. I won't be imprisoned for long."

I laughed and hurried down the steps to meet Adam. When I opened the door, he started to step inside. I put my hand against his chest to stop him. "It's almost six thirty," I said. "Why don't we get going?"

"Okay." He looked up toward the little surveillance camera and waved good-bye. Then he followed me to the car. "Maybe we can have dinner with Gabe again sometime. I really enjoyed it." He came around and opened the car door for me. "How are you feeling?"

I slid into the passenger seat. "I feel fine. And yes, we'll get together with Gabe again. You like him, don't you?"

"I really do. He's a great guy."

"Yes, he is."

On the way to the restaurant, Adam shared a little more about his group, Clowns for Christ. He'd been with the group for a couple of years. Started at his church as a way to cheer up sick children, it now had ten members who split events between two groups of five clowns each. As he talked about the men he worked with and the vision they shared, I could hear the compassion in his voice for hurting children. It touched my heart and made me feel even closer to him.

We pulled into the parking lot of the restaurant about ten minutes to seven. I didn't see Paula's car, but I wasn't surprised. I assumed her friend had driven. As we walked in the door, I immediately spotted Paula sitting in a booth against the wall. A man with blond hair sat next to her. Adam and I made our way through the crowded restaurant to join them. I secretly hoped our conversation wouldn't focus on the situation with Mabel. I was enjoying the freedom of not having to think about her. I didn't relish being thrown back into the fire.

"Hey, you!" Paula sang out as we approached.

"Hi," I answered while we scooted into the other side of the booth. "This is Adam," I said as soon as we were settled. "Adam, this is my best friend, Paula."

Paula stuck her hand out, her nails painted glossy black and decorated with some kind of silver symbols. Adam didn't seem to notice and shook her hand enthusiastically.

"Great to meet you," he said with a smile.

Paula winked at me. "He's cute, Hilde. Good job."

Adam laughed.

She let go of his hand and pointed to the man sitting next to her. "This is Martin. I told you about him, Hilde."

Martin was a nice-looking man with a ready smile. He shook hands with Adam. "Nice to meet both of you."

The waitress stepped up to ask us what we wanted to drink. We both ordered coffee and picked up our menus. The four of us discussed our choices. Paula and Martin settled on steak. I picked salmon, and Adam picked one of the restaurant's specialties—chicken fried steak with all the fixings.

"So, Hilde," Martin said after the waitress left with our orders, "Paula tells me you have questions about a body I transported."

"To be honest, Martin, I'm not pursuing it anymore. I turned my concerns over to her family. But if you have any information that might help them, I'd certainly be willing to hear it."

He shrugged. "I'm not sure if it will help them or not. As Paula probably told you, I work for River City Mortuary Service. We do lots of deliveries around town when a mortuary's own wagons are tied up. Last Monday I got called out to Druther's to pick up a body that needed to go to the coroner's office. I remember it because it's unusual to take someone from a funeral home to the coroner's. Usually it's the other way around. I always check the tags carefully, so I know it was this Winnemaker woman. I delivered her, and then on Wednesday I got called by Druther's to pick her up again, which I did."

He looked at me expectantly. I wasn't sure what he was waiting for.

"He's telling you it was the same body, Hilde. Druther's gave him a body, and he returned the same body. There weren't any mistakes. Ron was telling the truth."

I glanced at Adam, who looked a little uncomfortable. All the cards seemed to be stacked against me. Did *everyone* believe I was wrong about Mabel? Could they be right? There were still unanswered questions about Mabel's ring, my camera, and the fire at Druther's. But the bump on my head and my confusion over Martin's information were combining to stir up the beginnings of another headache. All I could think about were the pain pills back in my apartment. Maybe one more wouldn't be too bad. Right before I went to bed.

"I. . .I really don't want to talk about Mabel anymore," I said, trying to sound as nice as I could. "I will never believe that the woman whose hair I styled was the same woman I originally met at Druther's. And to be honest, I don't even care anymore. I'll let her family sort it out. I'm done."

"Do you really mean that, Hilde?" Paula asked.

I nodded too quickly. A dull pain throbbed behind my eyes. "Yes. I mean it." I picked up my glass of water and held it out. "Here's to never mentioning Mabel Winnemaker again." Three other glasses of water touched mine.

Paula broke out into a big smile. "Great. This is exactly why I wanted you to meet Martin. I knew he could reassure you about Ma. . .I mean, the person we're never going to mention again."

I was grateful to Paula. She really did have my best interests at heart. "Okay, now that 'she who cannot be named' is behind us, what shall we talk about?"

"There is one more thing I need to tell you that I think will also set your mind at ease," Paula said. "Gus says you really shouldn't worry about anything Ron might say about you. You wouldn't be the first person he's accused of improprieties. Some of the other directors have been caught in his crosshairs, too. He's not well liked, Hilde. If he does accuse you of anything, Gus plans to stand up for you. A good word from him has more weight than any allegations Ron might cook up."

I felt like a big weight had been lifted off my shoulders. "Thanks, Paula," I said with a sigh of relief. "And thank Gus for me, will you?"

For the next hour we discussed normal things like jobs and family. I found out that Paula had actually known Martin for a couple of years. He'd moved here from Arizona and has a motorcycle that isn't currently running. Leave it to Paula to date a motorcyclist without a motorcycle. I also discovered that Gus offered Paula a promotion. She is now a senior funeral director. I was thrilled for her, and she seemed pretty pleased with herself. Adam talked a little about his work, and I was relieved to find out he cares a little more about it than he'd previously let on. I could see that it isn't the business side of his job that appeals to him. It's the *people* side. Without mentioning names, he told a few funny stories about his clients, including one about an elderly woman who bakes him chocolate cakes when she makes money and bran muffins when her stocks go down. All in all, it was a very enjoyable evening. As time wore on, however, my headache got worse. I finally explained my fall and subsequent sore head. However, the revelation that Adam likes to dress up like a clown gave Paula a case of uncontrolled giggles.

"I'm glad you find my injury so humorous," I told her after another long bout of laughter.

She wiped her eyes and grinned at me. "I do. I really, really do. I'm sorry, but that has got to be one of the funniest things I've ever heard." At this, she took off again, joined by Martin and Adam. I tried to ignore them, but the silliness of the whole situation finally caught up with me. I couldn't help but laugh. For some reason, that sent all of them into hysterics.

We finally decided to leave before we were asked to. People were beginning to stare. Martin was nice enough to pick up the bill, even though I told him I should be treating him since he was there to help me. He wouldn't listen and took care of it anyway. I'd started to like him. He actually had manners and appeared to be very respectful of Paula—something she wasn't used to. He helped her into her coat before putting on his leather jacket. I was mildly amused to see an insignia for a motorcycle club on the front. I hoped that even if he did get his motorcycle fixed, he wouldn't take Paula out on it. I distrust motorcycles. Working in funeral homes teaches you something about them—and it isn't good.

We said good night in the parking lot, with Paula promising to call me. I tried not to smile when Martin escorted her to his vehicle. RIVER CITY MORTUARY SERVICE was painted in white letters on the side of his black van. Not very subtle. A couple of people in the parking lot stared at them as they got into the vehicle, but it didn't seem to bother Paula at all.

I waved good-bye once more as we pulled out of the parking lot and headed back to Eden.

"I like your friend," Adam said when we got out onto the street. "She's very honest, isn't she?"

"Yes she is. I like honest people." I told him about Paula's background and how I was trying to help her find her way to God.

He smiled at me when I finished. "I have no doubt you'll be able to help her, Hilde. You're not judgmental. Instead you're showing her the love of God through your love for her. There are a lot of Christians who need to learn how to do that."

We didn't talk much the rest of the way home. Adam knew my head was really hurting again. He walked me to the front door and promised to call me. I climbed the stairs quietly, not wanting to attract any attention. I probably didn't need to worry. Mrs. Hudson and Minnie were giggling like schoolgirls in the kitchen. I was glad to hear Mrs. Hudson was having so much fun. I was pretty sure she wasn't going to enjoy it tomorrow when I told her about Derek's special tea blend.

I opened the door to my apartment and turned on the light. I could tell right away that something wasn't right. Two of the drawers in my dresser were open slightly, and things on my table had been moved around. Someone had been in my room. A quick search didn't reveal anything missing—except the music box Gabe had given me.

CHAPTER ⫟⫟⫟⫟ THIRTEEN

I didn't say anything to Mrs. Hudson before I left for church the next morning. I'd decided to confront her with the evidence of Derek's business dealings when I got back from my mother's. Would she be convinced he was the one stealing our possessions? I wasn't sure, but I was fairly certain I could prove it. An image of him helping me to my room when Adam brought me back from my unfortunate accident had broken through my drug-induced haze. He'd been coming from Minnie's room; I was certain of it. A quick call to Adam confirmed my suspicions. I sat through church praying that God would help me share the information in a way that wouldn't hurt Mrs. Hudson and would somehow help Derek. I'd also have to tell Gabe about the music box. I hoped he wouldn't be too upset.

It was a little after one when I got to my mother's. I've never gotten used to driving into her long, curved driveway. Her place is huge—ten times the size of the home I grew up in. The only thing on Mom's property that reminds me of our little place is the two-car garage that sits on one side of her property. It's about the same size as our old house.

I parked the car and climbed the front steps to the large double doors under the Southern-like pillars on each side of the porch. Then I rang the bell. It seemed odd to have to ring the doorbell at my mother's house, but she'd made it clear that she didn't want me to "just walk in like I own the place."

The front door was pulled open, and Mom stood there like she was welcoming party guests into her mansion. She still had on her clothes from church. A black suit with white pearls. Actually, she looked gorgeous. Not that I planned to tell her that.

"Come on in, Hilde!" Her clear voice echoed in the huge front hall. I followed her into the kitchen, which was toward the back of the house. The aroma was unmistakable. It had been so long since I'd had my mother's chili that I had problems actually recalling the taste. But the smell took me back as if it had been just yesterday since I'd melted cheddar cheese and sprinkled chopped onions on top of a steaming bowl of Naomi Higgins's incredible chili con carne.

Mom stirred the big pot on the stove a couple of times and then turned to look at me. Her mouth dropped open. "You're wearing the coat I gave you."

I nodded and plopped down at the kitchen table. I pulled off my jacket and draped it over the chair next to me. "The other one finally gave up the ghost. I tried this one on, and I liked it. Thank you."

Her expression was classic. You'd have thought I told her I'd discovered the cure for cancer through eating SPAM®. She couldn't have been more surprised.

"Perhaps you should try on some of the other clothes I bought you," she said, looking me up and down. "I might be right about them as well."

I started to respond with something snarky, but I stopped myself just in the nick of time. "Maybe so, Mom. We'll see." It was definitely time to change the subject. "So, how was church today?"

"Hildegard Higgins, I don't appreciate your snide remarks about my church," she snapped. "I'm going to change my clothes. I would appreciate it if you would stir the chili a couple of times while I'm gone. And for heaven's sake, don't let it burn."

With that, she twirled on her heels and exited—leaving me with chili duty and a kick in the teeth. How in the world did an innocent question about church end up as an attack? Boy, things had really gone south with my mom, even more than I'd realized. I got up and checked the chili. It looked great, but I stirred it anyway. If she came back and found it scorched, she would interpret it as some kind of personal affront.

While I stared at the bubbling mixture, I couldn't rid myself of a nagging feeling that had been pulling at me ever since I'd crawled out of bed. It was like I'd forgotten something important, but I couldn't quite grab it. Usually the things I couldn't remember were things I'd heard—not things I'd seen. But this time, it was as if pictures were floating around in my brain that I couldn't piece together. What was it? I thought back to dinner the night before. Martin's information hadn't helped or hurt anything. Or had it? There was something about what he said—or was there something else that had ignited this uneasiness inside me? As I stirred the chili, I also tried to stir up the images that were moving through my brain like unconnected flash cards. But nothing made sense.

"For goodness' sakes, Hilde. I didn't tell you to turn it into mush." My mother's sharp rebuke startled me, and I flipped the spoon out of the pot, spraying chili on the stove, on the floor, and on me.

"Oh, sorry," I said, looking down at chili that dripped down the side of my left shoe and onto the floor. "I was thinking about something else."

With a big sigh, my mother came over and took the spoon from my hand. "It's okay, Hildegard. It's what I get for giving you something to do. Just sit down. I'll finish up."

She had changed into casual slacks and a shimmery white blouse. Only my mother would wear white while making chili. Of course, she wouldn't get a drop on her clothing. I, on the other hand, am a magnet for stains. I shrugged and sat down at the table. She handed me a damp dish towel so I could clean myself up.

"What were you thinking about?" she asked as she mopped up the mess I'd made. "You looked like you were miles and miles away when I came into the kitchen."

I updated her briefly on the situation with Mabel. "So I guess it's out of my hands. Mabel's family is in charge now, as they should be. And Ron Druther seems to have his own problems. Frankly, I don't think he'll cause me any complications. Even if he does tell any of the other directors about my supposed thievery, Paula doesn't think they'll believe him. Turns out he's not too popular among his colleagues."

Mom took some bowls out of the refrigerator and set them on the table: cheese, chopped onions, diced jalapeños, and sour cream. Then she grabbed a small bowl off the counter. Oyster crackers. My mouth began to water. My mother's chili recipe was exceptional—just like everything else about her. Of course, I had a pretty good chili recipe myself, but I didn't think my mom would appreciate the main ingredient.

"Something still bothers you about this situation, doesn't it, Hilde?"

I broke my gaze away from the chili accompaniments spread out in front of me. It almost sounded like she was interested. Homemade chili and concern for me together in one afternoon? I wasn't certain I could bear it.

I nodded. "It's like I've remembered something important, but it's just a bunch of images that don't make sense." I sighed. "Maybe I'm just hungry. I don't know. When do we eat?"

Mom took two bowls out of her cabinet and scooped chili into them. Then she carried them to the table. "I guess we eat now. Would you like to say grace?"

Every time my mother asked me if I wanted to say grace, I had to push back an almost overwhelming desire to smile at her and say, "Grace." But having tried it once, I'd discovered she didn't see the humor in it like I did. I bowed my head and thanked God for the food and for the wonderful fellowship my mother and I would be sharing today. The second part of that prayer was said in faith, of course.

I'd just started dressing up my chili with cheese and onions when my mother put down her spoon with a bang and said a word I'd never heard come out of her mouth before. Startled, I looked up to see tears in her eyes. Goodness, what faux pas had I committed to evoke this kind of response? The wrong cheese to onion ratio? Or was it that I had rejected her jalapeños?

"Mother, what in the world?"

"Hilde, after what happened at the hospital yesterday, I've come to the realization that I've made several mistakes in my relationship with you." She picked up her napkin and dabbed at her eyes so that her tears wouldn't mess up her mascara.

"I don't understand. What mistakes do you mean?" I could think of at least twenty without breaking a sweat. But what my mother saw as "mistakes" were anyone's guess. Was it allowing me to leave school? To become a hairdresser? To work in funeral homes with dead people "for crying out loud"? Or perhaps it was simply the mistake of being born in the first place. With my mother, anything was possible.

She straightened up as if trying to find the courage to

continue. Uh-oh. This wasn't going to be good. My mother never worried about anything she said. I had a strong feeling I wasn't going to like whatever came next.

"I. . .I want to apologize to you, Hilde. I realized when I saw you lying in the hospital that I'd done you a great disservice by not telling you why you are afraid of clowns. At the time, I felt you'd successfully blocked certain aspects of your illness as a protective device. I didn't want to disrupt that. But I realize now that fear and pain can't really be locked away inside us; they just sit in our subconscious and cause other problems."

To say I was shocked was a huge understatement. But what happened next was even more astonishing. My mother reached over and took my hand in hers.

"It's my fault that we haven't been closer, Hilde. When your dad left, it shattered something inside me. You see, I loved him very much."

Tears streaked down her cheeks, and she didn't even try to save her mascara. This in itself was unusual, but hearing her apologize and make an attempt to share her true feelings touched something deep inside my soul. I felt my own eyes get wet.

"When I understood that you'd been keeping your fears hidden away, I had to face the fact that I've been doing the same thing all these years. And it hasn't helped either one of us. So"—she squeezed my hand—"I wanted to tell you how sorry I am and admit to you that I've been nursing a lot of anger for a long time, and I think I've been pushing you away without meaning to. Probably to protect me from more pain." She finally wiped her tear-stained face. "I want you to understand that my job became so important to me because it was a place where I could hide from how devastated I really was. It was wrong. You come first, Hilde. Anyway, you're going to start coming first. I hope to mend our relationship— as long as it isn't too late."

I couldn't say anything. My throat was tight with emotion. Mom handed me a tissue from a box sitting on the table.

"It's not too late," I blubbered. "And I'm sorry, too. Sometimes I say awful things to you. I don't mean them; they just kind of pop out of my mouth."

"I understand, sweetheart. I've been doing the same thing. Maybe the first thing we need to concentrate on is what we say to each other. I'll try to not criticize your hair or your clothes—and maybe you can quit saying negative things about my church. And we could both stop picking at each other about our jobs."

"I really don't dislike your church, Mother. I like it very much. Maybe if I quit calling it the 'church of the frozen chosen,' you could quit calling mine that 'happy clappy church.'"

She nodded. "I think that's doable. And for the record, I'm pleased that you've found a place where you feel you belong. And there's nothing wrong with being expressive in your worship."

I smiled. "I'll let you in on a secret, Mom. I love the songs we sing in church, but sometimes I wish they'd sing some of the old hymns I learned when I was younger. I enjoy them, too."

She squeezed my hand and then let it go. "There is one more thing I must tell you, Hilde. It's difficult for me to say, but I know now that I must."

My insides turned cold. Okay, this must be the part about the terminal disease. Was it me, or was it her? Fear danced the merengue in my intestines. "What is it, Mother?"

She sighed and shook her head. "Orange. I know why you hate the color orange."

"You do?" Well, thank God the fatal disease thing was out of the mix. I was curious about this newest disclosure, but I also hoped it wasn't as traumatic as facing my inner clowns had been.

Mom stared down at her clasped hands. "You started hating orange the day your father left with that woman."

"I—I don't understand," I said. "What does orange have to do with anything?" Even before she responded, pictures of that day jumped into my mind. Pictures I'd kept behind a mental door—locked safely away. My father, leaving with his suitcase, going out to a car where his new girlfriend waited. The woman he'd chosen over us—the woman with the bright orange sports car. I guess the look on my face told my mother everything she needed to know.

"I'm sorry, Hilde," she said softly. "I think you connected

your dad's leaving with that woman's car. I was never absolutely certain about it, but with the way your mind works, if you just now remembered the color of her car, I think it's obvious that your subconscious has kept that memory at bay to protect you." She wiped her face again. "The day your father left was the worst day of my life. I'd hoped that since you were young, it wouldn't be as hurtful for you. Obviously, I was wrong. Maybe it's time we were honest about our pain and found healing together."

"That sounds like a good idea, Mom," I said. "But I don't think I can take any more emotional upheaval for today. Maybe we could go at it again another time."

She smiled and nodded. "I have to agree. I feel rather wrung out, and I'm sure my makeup is a mess."

"I kind of like it when you don't look perfect," I said with a grin.

"Honestly, Hilde," she said. "Why in the world. . ." She stopped herself and started to laugh. "Okay, this will take some practice. I'm afraid we both suffer from a disability we could call *sharp-tongue-itis.*"

I giggled. "I think your diagnosis is correct, doctor. Is there a cure?"

"I think a good dose of patience, love, and trust will work wonders," she said. "Do you think you'll be able to stick to the medication I've prescribed?"

"Yes, I think we both will." I could feel my eyes tearing up again. Enough of that. "I also think we need to heat up this chili a little."

Mom picked up my bowl and carried it to the microwave. "I can do that." She stuck the bowl inside and watched it rotate. "You know, when you were younger, you used to spend a lot of time reading. I think you were hiding from the hurt of losing your dad by diving into someone else's life—someone else's story."

"That's entirely possible. I still read a lot, and to be honest, I've noticed that when I'm stressed, I'll head for a book before anything else."

She smiled. "Do you recall the summer you decided to read every novel Agatha Christie ever wrote? We sure spent a lot of time at the library, looking through the mystery section."

"Yeah, I do remember." I knew I sounded as distracted as I felt. That feeling was back, the pictures running together in my mind.

My mom didn't seem to notice. She carried my bowl over to the table and placed it in front of me. "What do you want to drink? I made a pitcher of iced tea, but if you'd rather have something hot. . ."

"No. Iced tea is fine," I said, reaching for the pitcher. Instead of grabbing the handle, my hand bumped up against it, and the container nearly toppled over. Mom grabbed it just in time.

"Thank you, Hilde," she said, "but I've already been baptized. A second time isn't necessary."

In that instant, all the little pictures in my mind came together and formed an image. I was looking at something I'd never expected to see.

I stared at my mother with astonishment. "Mom, I need to make a phone call."

"What are you talking about? What's wrong?"

"I need to call Adam so he can contact his friend at the police department. Mabel Winnemaker was murdered. I know who did it, and I'm pretty sure I know why."

CHAPTER FOURTEEN

We laid Mabel Winnemaker to rest Wednesday afternoon. After leaving the cemetery, the mourners headed to Eden. Mabel's story had touched Mrs. Hudson and Minnie so much they'd offered to host a dinner for her friends and family. Only three of us knew that there was another reason she had extended such a gracious invitation. Telling her about Derek had upset her, but in the end, she'd been very grateful. The missing items, pawned for drug money, had been located and would be returned to their respective owners after Derek's sentencing. A very repentant young man had helped the police find everything that had been stolen. Although his immediate family didn't appear to want much to do with him, his aunt hadn't forsaken him. Encouraged by her love, Derek seemed to turn a corner. I was praying for him as were the other tenants at Mrs. Hudson's boardinghouse, along with Adam, Gabe, and my mother. With that kind of prayer support, I was confident he had a good chance to turn out okay.

At six o'clock, a large group gathered around the table in Mrs. Hudson's kitchen. Gabe said a prayer over our meal, his last words followed by a chorus of *Amens*.

"So you were at your mother's house when you realized my grandmother had actually been murdered?"

I passed the bowl of mashed potatoes to William Winnemaker. His dark brown eyes fastened on me with interest.

"Yes. As I told you, I have a photographic memory. It stored all kinds of pictures in my mind, but until my mother mentioned Agatha Christie and being 'baptized,' they had no connection."

"I should have realized there was only one person who could have switched those bodies," Paula said. "I can't believe I was so dense."

I shook my head. "Don't be silly. There's no way you could have known. Even I overlooked the most obvious clue as to what really happened."

"And what was that?" Isaiah smiled at me, but I'm pretty sure I'm not the one who put that big grin on his face. I'd called Ida Mae and asked her to join us for dinner. Isaiah and the elderly bookstore owner hit it off immediately. Who knew that Isaiah loved to read almost as much as Ida Mae? When Mrs. Hudson apologized to Isaiah for suspecting him of stealing, he told her the real reason he disappears every day. Having been married over forty years, he's so lonely for his wife that he spends almost every day at the cemetery, talking to her tombstone. With a little push from God, maybe Isaiah will start using some of his time to talk to the living. Even though they just met, the glances and quick smiles going back and forth between him and Ida Mae are indications of a nice friendship—if not something more someday.

I sighed. "Now it seems so obvious. If Mabel number one and Mabel number two were different people, and if they weren't mixed up at the funeral home, the only place they could have been switched was at the coroner's office."

"And that pointed you to Martin?" Adam asked.

"Yes. Mortuary service employees have keys to get inside when the office is closed. I never suspected that the mix-up occurred there, because the coroner's office is known for their efficiency and caution. But sneaking in after hours made it possible for Martin to switch Mabel with another elderly woman who wasn't claimed by anyone. No one caught it because he did it before the autopsy."

"I can't believe that other poor woman had no one to protect her," Minnie said sadly. "How could a human being die and have absolutely no one who cares enough to make sure they have a decent burial and a little respect?"

"It's sad," I said, "but especially among the homeless, bodies are often brought in without any kind of identification. Still, it was a lucky break to find someone who resembled Mabel so closely at the time they needed her."

"That *was* a lucky break," Paula said. "What if there hadn't been another body available?"

I shook my head. "I have no idea."

"I guess it was my request for an autopsy that started this whole thing," William said. "I wasn't actually suspicious about Grandmother's death. I just wanted to make certain everything was done by the book. I think it was the guilt of not being here when she died. I had no idea it would set all this in motion."

"Of course you didn't," I said. "The killers thought they'd committed the perfect crime. An overdose of insulin stopped Mabel's heart, and a doctor who was already expecting her health to fail made it easy for them to create a death no one would find suspicious. They planned to have Mabel gone and buried before you ever got to town. But when you ordered the autopsy, they knew they could be discovered. That's when they called on their old friend Martin for help."

"One thing I don't understand," Mom said. "Why didn't Alfred and Edith just wait until Mabel died of natural causes? They were set to inherit a great deal of money. It probably wouldn't have been that long."

I shook my head. "They couldn't risk it. Somehow, Mabel found out that they'd learned about the inheritance. It was supposed to be a secret."

"That's right," William said. "As far as I knew, their interest in taking care of Grandmother was completely altruistic. I didn't want that to change. I felt that keeping the knowledge of the will to ourselves was the right thing to do. But now, I'm certain that getting her money was their goal from the beginning. Quite a few pieces of my grandmother's jewelry are missing. I've also discovered that the money from her Social Security checks probably went straight into their pockets. Grandmother's checking account was almost empty." He shrugged. "I don't know exactly how they found out about the inheritance, but my lawyer admitted one of his secretaries called the house several months ago. At the time, she didn't realize that Alfred and Edith weren't supposed to be contacted. I'll bet that's when they learned of the will's existence."

"When Mabel realized they were taking her for all she was worth," I said, "she wanted to send a warning to William—something to let him know she needed his help. That's when she wrote the letter I found inside her book. Unfortunately, she never got to mail it. Somehow, Edith and Alfred found out that Mabel was on to them. They knew their windfall was in jeopardy and they had to kill her before the will was changed."

"Could they have seen the letter?" Ida Mae asked. "Maybe that's what alerted them to Mabel's suspicions."

"I don't think so," I said. "It was still inside the book they gave me. I doubt they ever saw it. We may never know how they found out that Mabel didn't trust them anymore. I suspect the missing jewelry and the lack of money in her checking account helped to point her to the truth. As far as the letter, though, even if they'd found it, they wouldn't have understood the hidden message Mabel had put there just for William."

William nodded. "When I was a boy, my grandmother and I had a secret code we created for fun. We'd write letters to each other. Every other capitalized letter signified a word that was part of the message. Proper names and the first letters of sentences didn't count. She was trying to get a note to me, using that old code of ours."

"Somehow, Hilde figured it out," Gabe said.

"That's right," I said. "On Sunday, when Mom brought up Agatha Christie, that letter popped clearly into my mind. I started to think about how some of the words were capitalized incorrectly. At first I'd attributed it to poor eyesight, but then I got to thinking about it. Edith said that Mabel read every day. If she could see the words in regular books, then her vision couldn't have been that bad. And since she was very well read, she shouldn't have made that many mistakes. Also, her use of the word *mysterious* seemed unusual. Once I started to see some of the other capitalized words in my mind, I realized Mabel wanted William to think of *The Mysterious Affair at Styles* by Agatha Christie. After that, it was easy to figure out that she was trying to send him a message."

"I know that story," Mom said. "It's about a woman who is poisoned because of her will."

"That's right, Mom," I said. "And the name of the murderer is Alfred. Mabel was trying to tell William that she suspected she was in danger from her nephew."

"That was the Christie novel that introduced Hercule Poirot, by the way," Adam interjected.

I looked at him with surprise.

"Hey, I'm not a total dummy when it comes to mysteries. Just because I'm a stockbroker doesn't mean I don't read."

I chuckled at his injured expression. "Okay. You can read. I'm even more impressed."

"Hilde," Ida Mae said, "I understand everything you've explained, but I still don't see how you knew this Martin person was involved—beyond realizing that the bodies were probably changed at the coroner's office."

"Actually, Martin was involved from the very beginning. He started up a whirlwind romance with Gwen so he'd have access to Druther's. That enabled him to make the substitution. I actually saw Martin's black van the morning I went to work on Mabel. He was there—hanging around to make sure no one noticed anything was wrong. His substitute had made it through the rest of her preparation without raising suspicions. He probably thought he was home free. Then I showed up. He was in Gwen's office when I knocked on her door. Since she was trying to keep her relationship with him secret because of Ron's feelings for her, he scooted out the back door. He came inside through the alley door and hid in the room where the body was waiting. He wanted to make sure the plan he'd hatched with his accomplices had worked. But when he heard me on the phone with Paula, raising a stink about the body not being Mabel's, he knew he had to do something to discredit me. He put her diamond ring in my purse and took my camera, removing any proof that the woman on the table wasn't Mabel Winnemaker. Then he left, certain no one would believe my claims."

"How did he gain access to the ring?" Isaiah asked. "I know the funeral home kept my wife's jewelry under lock and key."

"Someone left the keys out on a counter where anyone could have gotten to them. That's how Martin got his hands on the ring, and that's why Ron Druther thought I'd had the chance to steal it."

"But there had to be more than just the van that pointed you to him," Ida Mae insisted. "What else tipped you off?"

"There were several things." I leaned over and picked up my purse. After rifling through it a minute, I pulled out an ink pen. I held up the black pen with its silver writing. "It's from the Flying Demon Motorcycle Club in Phoenix, Arizona. I had to have picked it up in Gwen's office when I was writing down my next appointment with them. It's the motorcycle club Martin belongs to. I saw the insignia on his coat at the restaurant Saturday night. Also, Gwen told me she was going on vacation where it was warm and there were palm trees. Of course, she could have been talking about several different locations, but when I realized that Martin had come from Phoenix, the pen and Gwen's words all pointed to him. Martin was the friend Gwen was going out of town with. Martin says he really cared for her. Who knows? But when she started getting suspicious about Mabel not being Mabel, he began to worry. When she told him she was meeting with me, he panicked and hit her. He says he didn't mean to kill her, but when he realized she was dead, he started the fire to cover up his actions."

"Then when Hilde remembered that Alfred and Edith were also from Phoenix, she realized what had happened," Adam said. "The Winnemakers needed a way to keep Mabel from being autopsied. So they called their old friend Martin and asked for a favor in exchange for a cut of the inheritance money."

"How large was the inheritance?" Mom asked.

"Half a million dollars," William answered. "Grandmother wanted to make certain Alfred and Edith were well taken care of."

"So instead of inheriting all that money, they're going away for murder and accessory to murder," Mom said. "Do you know who administered the insulin overdose?"

"Edith says Alfred did it. Alfred blames Edith." I sighed. "Of course, they're not the only ones who will be charged with murder."

"You mean Martin," Paula said.

"Yes. I can actually testify that he was at the scene of the fire on the night Gwen died. Again, Mom jogged my memory the other day when she mentioned my almost spilling a pitcher of tea. Martin used the exact phrase when I ran into him at Starbucks the night of the fire. Although I was in such a hurry I didn't look at his face, I remembered the insignia on his coat. He wore the same jacket when we went out to dinner.

He was at Starbucks, making certain Druther's burned to the ground. Thankfully, he didn't remember me when Paula introduced us. I guess we were both pretty preoccupied that night."

"Martin cut a deal with the DA and is singing like a bird," William said. "He'll probably spend most of his life in prison."

"He certainly sold his dear friends Edith and Alfred down the river," Gabe said. "Not much loyalty among that group."

"I hope he gets put away for a long, long time," I said. "No matter what he says, I don't believe he cared about Gwen at all. He was only using her."

"And me," Paula said. "He only showed an interest in me so he could find out if you were still a threat to him. You'd convinced Alfred and Edith that you weren't going to pursue the situation any longer, but he wanted to hear it straight from the horse's mouth. That's why he cozied up to me and finagled a meeting with you. Once he'd convinced himself you were out of the picture and he was safe, he planned to drop me like a hot potato."

Gabe cleared his throat and frowned at me. "If he'd determined you were dangerous to him and his upcoming windfall, he might have made plans to *accidentally* get you out of the way as well. I think you were in more danger than you realized, Hilde."

"Talking to Alfred and Edith probably kept me out of serious trouble," I acknowledged. "They figured that since I was out of the picture and the substitute Mabel was gone and buried, they were home free."

"And of course they made up that story about out-of-town relatives," William said, "so they could bury Grandmother before I got here. They didn't want to give me any chance to see the body before it was buried."

"Yes," I agreed. "They thought they'd tied up every loose end."

"I haven't had time to tell you, Hilde," Paula said with a smile, "but Gus offered Ron a job."

"Did he take it?"

She shook her head. "No. He hates the mortuary business. Always did. He's going to do what he's always wanted to do."

"And that is?"

She giggled. "Study veterinary medicine."

"He wants to be a veterinarian?" I said, laughing. "I hope he's nicer to animals than he is to people. But what about his losses from the fire?"

"Actually, Gus has been looking to expand. He's buying the property and cleaning it up. Then he'll build a second funeral home there. Property values have skyrocketed since Ron's family bought that plot of land. Believe it or not, he'll walk away with a nice little chunk of change. As long as no one sues him, he should be fine. Right now, it doesn't look like any of the families involved in the fire are willing to pursue legal action." She grinned triumphantly. "I think he's going to come out just fine."

"Good. That poor man really didn't have any idea what was going on with Mabel. He must have thought I was losing my mind."

"Well, he doesn't think you're bonkers now," Paula said. "I'm sure he's grateful that you didn't give up. He may have lost his building—but I think he's gained a chance at a new life."

"Well," Minnie said, "I can hardly believe how everything came together the way it did. It's a real murder mystery. Just like you'd read in a book!"

"Except that this wasn't just a story," I said. "Mabel and Gwen were real people. I'll miss Gwen, and I'll always wish I could have gotten to know Mabel."

William smiled. "She would have liked you very much, Hilde."

"So I take it Mabel's no longer missing?" Isaiah asked.

I nodded. "The coroner helped us find her. She was buried in an unmarked grave without any kind of identification."

"But she's where she should be now," William said. "And there's a chance that the other woman will be identified, too. Detectives found Hilde's camera in Martin's apartment. With those pictures, at least there's the possibility of uncovering her real identity."

Gabe reached over and patted my shoulder. "Someday," he said softly, "you and Mabel will sit down and talk this whole thing out. What a wonderful day that will be."

I smiled. That was something I looked forward to. As everyone began to talk about other things, I gazed around the table. My mother was asking Gabe about his interest in antiques and tea.

Mrs. Hudson and Minnie quickly turned their attention elsewhere. The subject of tea was a sore point. They'd been absolutely horrified to find out that the herbs they'd thought Derek had purchased for his aunt as a surprise was actually marijuana. It certainly explained the evening of uncontrolled giggling and frivolity that had ensued after brewing and drinking tea containing some of the illegal substance. I suspected there wouldn't be any more *stinky tea* coming from Mrs. Hudson's kitchen for a long, long time.

My mother's laughter at something Gabe said washed over me like a healing balm. Ever since we'd had our heart-to-heart talk, things have been better between us. Not perfect. Just better. The most remarkable thing is the look on her face now. There's a freedom—a quiet joy that hadn't been there for a long time—a fruit of the Spirit that's been inside her, waiting to come out. We've both learned an important lesson: Allowing hurt and anger to quench the fruit God has given us can keep us from being everything He has created us to be. I'm not sure yet just who the real Hilde Higgins is—but I know she's not the insecure little girl who watched her father drive out of her life in an orange car. Finding my true identity may take some time, but I intend to make that journey hand in hand with my real Father. The One who will never desert me. And now that Mom and I are both on the road to healing, I have every hope that we can have the kind of relationship I've always wanted.

My mother and I aren't the only people who have changed. Gabe is a different person, too. His bitter-old-man facade is gone. However, there are still secrets swirling around him. I wonder if I'll ever really know him—or if our relationship will always stay confined to the boundaries he's set to protect himself.

Then there is Paula, who at the moment was trying to answer Minnie's questions about funerals. Minnie didn't understand why she couldn't be tossed into a hole in the ground in the backyard when she died, and Mrs. Hudson was trying to get both of them to stop talking about it. Paula has actually agreed to go to church with me. . .*sometime*. It's vague, but it's a step in the right direction. I understand her better now. She's holding on to hurt the way Mom and I did. Someday she'll have to learn that feelings buried alive never die—they just find other ways to wiggle out and mess up your life. Paula's wounds show up in false religions and in her choice of men—neither one bringing her true freedom.

And then there's Adam. My fingers closed around the slip of paper he'd given me the night before. It was the fortune from our very first date. *The love you've been waiting for is closer than you think.* He'd told me he might give it back to me someday—and he has. We've both admitted to strong feelings for each other. I'm not sure if I'm really in love, but

I'm certainly willing to find out. I'm excited to see what the future will bring.

I also returned his fortune to him. He laughed when he reread it. "I have no doubt having you in my life will bring the unexpected, Hilde," he said. Then he'd kissed me.

I cut off a little piece of my meat loaf and held it down toward my feet. Watson took it gently from my fingers. Adam rescued him from the pound just in time. Although Mrs. Hudson has given Adam permission to bring Watson with him for visits, he can't live here with me. Even if she would change the rules, going up and down the stairs is too hard for an older dog with asthma. Happily, Adam's landlord has allowed Watson to move in. Since Adam lives in a duplex and has a fenced yard, it's the perfect place for Mabel's dog to live out the rest of his life. Adam and Watson have bonded, and it's cute to watch them together. I know Mabel would be pleased.

A glance around the table revealed an odd but happy group. Tonight we'd all been brought together because of Mabel. I whispered a little thank-you to her, confident that somehow she heard me.

I leaned over and asked my mother if she wanted another helping of meat loaf. She smiled and nodded. Then she went back to her conversation with Gabe. It would be awhile before I trusted our newfound relationship enough to admit that tonight's main dish was my creation. I laughed softly as I cut off a slice and put it on her plate.

SPAM® ON A STICK

1 egg
¼ cup milk
1 package of saltine crackers, crushed
½ can of corn, drained
1 cup flour
Salt to taste
Pepper to taste
1 can of SPAM® Classic
Skewers

Beat egg and milk together. Set aside. In another bowl, mix crackers and corn together. Put flour in another dish. Add salt and pepper as desired. Cut SPAM® Classic into whatever size you want. Cubes or rectangles work well. Dip pieces into the egg and milk then into the flour. Repeat. Roll coated SPAM® pieces in crackers and corn. Fry the pieces in hot oil and then stick them on your skewers! You're ready to enjoy SPAM® on a stick!

Recipe by Linda Frye whose father, John, taught her everything she knows about SPAM®!

Nancy Mehl lives in Wichita, Kansas, with her husband, Norman, and her son, Danny. She's authored nine books and is currently at work on two new series for Barbour Publishing.

All of Nancy's novels have an added touch—something for your spirit as well as your soul. "I welcome the opportunity to share my faith through my writing," Nancy says. "It's a part of me and of everything I think or do. God is number one in my life. I wouldn't be writing at all if I didn't believe that this is what He's called me to do. I hope everyone who reads my books will walk away with the most important message I can give them: God is good, and He loves you more than you can imagine. He has a good plan especially for *your* life, and there is nothing you can't overcome with His help."

You can find out more about Nancy by visiting her Web site at: www.nancymehl.com.

Other books by Nancy Mehl

Cozy in Kansas
Simple Secrets

THE HARMONY SERIES
Simple Secrets